ANCIENT CITIES OF INDIA

*A retelling of the history of select ancient
cities of undivided India*

SAYAN BHATTACHARYA

Become
Shakespeare
.com

First published in 2019 by

Becomeshakespeare.com

Wordit Content Design & Editing Services Pvt Ltd
Unit - 26, Building A -1, Nr Wadala RTO,
Wadala (East), Mumbai 400037, India
T: +91 8080226699

Wordit Art Fund helps deserving authors publish their work
by providing monetary support. To apply for funding, please
visit us at www.BecomeShakespeare.com

ISBN - 978-93-88930-13-0

Acknowledgements and credits

Ancient Cities of India was first conceptualized and written as a blog series in the Blogchatter A2Z blogging challenge in April 2018. I am grateful to my friends at Team Blogchatter for the opportunity and for giving *Ancient Cities of India* so much love as the series unfolded in the blog space. From accepting the theme of history and mythology combination, to ensuring widespread readership, to highlighting the stories through their various events on social media, viz., the dramatic book reading excerpt sessions, the Blogchatter Team provided the much-needed impetus and confidence that was required to convert the blog series into a paperback. Thank you, Team Blogchatter!

I will always be thankful to my fellow bloggers in the Blogchatter A2Z challenge and beyond, who took time out to read *Ancient Cities of India* and share feedback. Their comments and encouragement have gone a long way in helping me to construct this book, so thank you my fellow bloggers. I am happy to include some of your words of encouragement and appreciation which you had shared on social media, in the pages of this book.

To the reviewers of *Ancient Cities of India*, who not only read the book but also went ahead to review it on their blogs and websites, I owe you heartfelt thanks. Your reviews have not only encouraged and delighted me but have also ensured that the book reaches a lot of readers. Thank you for your kind words and your reviews of *Ancient Cities of India*, some of which I have included in the book.

My publishers' team, especially Pooja and Sameer from *BecomeShakespeare.com* for bearing with me patiently and obliging my requests, as I took my time with the manuscript and cover design of the book.

A big 'Thank You' to my dear friend Aravind Krishnan of Thiruvananthapuram, for being the reader and audience of my first drafts of the stories in *Ancient Cities of India*, and for his suggestions, inspiration and encouragement in my research and preparation of the book. I am equally grateful for Aravind's active participation in getting the cover design of the book coordinated and done to perfection.

Finally, my thanks and gratitude to you all for ensuring that *Ancient Cities of India* now sees the light of day!

Excerpts from Book Reviews of *Ancient Cities of India* by popular bloggers

"… *'Ancient Cities of India'* is an interesting read for people having a proclivity for history and mythology. It is a well-researched book and the author has done an outstanding job in bringing about some captivating facts about our country and its roots…

I loved the idea of keeping the book crisp yet informative. This would attract readers who might not want to get into the details of the archaeological facts but might be interested in giving it a read for mere knowledge. Another striking feature of the book is, it is listed in alphabetical order and it must have been a challenging job for the author to dig out information of the cities named accordingly. The author has done a commendable job in compiling information from various sources and bringing it out in his own writing style.

This book represents the country's historical past, traditions and rich culture which is depicted by the majestic temples and the beautiful cities. The author also pens about the rise and fall of various kingdoms in ancient times. I liked the author's style of writing and how his descriptions lead to a picturesque view of the cities like Hastinapur, Bairat, Lahore, Multan, Varanasi and many more.

The author beautifully brings to light the facts about our

rich cultural history which is unknown to many. He also very remarkably compiled his incredible research into one comprehensive book. This book will surely serve as a reference work for history lovers and an interesting read for everybody else and thus, *'Ancient Cities of India'* gets a thumbs-up from me."

- *Review Post dated 23 June 2018, by popular literary blogger **Rashi Roy** on her blog www.royrashi.blogspot.com*

"... *'Ancient Cities of India'* by Sayan Bhattacharya is an absorbing read. A map would be helpful, to keep the cities straight, specially for geographically challenged people like me. There are many interesting nuggets of information, about the cities in our rich past...

If like me, your notions of mythology are a little foggy, this book will set you to rights...

Myth and history meet seamlessly, where Sayan tells us of archaeologists finding proof of a submerged city where Dwarka was thought to exist...

Sayan seems a sleuth, as he talks about sifting through different versions of history, to determine which one seems most accurate. Want to know why Hastinapur is called that? If your Hindi is none too strong, like mine, you'll appreciate this detailed narrative.

The mythological tales around Indraprastha are also engaging. I didn't know Karna had a son! Kannauj is the short form of Kanyakubja- girl hunchbacks. Read the book for the story behind the name. The chapter on Multan is also interesting- about the lost Sun temple. And how priests carried idols to Haridwar after the Partition.

The adventure of the Kohinoor diamond is riveting. The tales around Sravasti too. "Buddha is said to have performed miracles in Sravasti, including the very famous *'twin miracle'* where simultaneously he had fire coming out of his shoulders and streams of water from his feet, thus representing the control of opposite elements of nature within his own self."

It's great to learn about the history of India- time traveled back to ancient times. Truth is stranger than fiction, and this book is more interesting than many novels…"

- *Review post dated 16 June 2018, by popular blogger **Nupur Maskara,** on her blog https://www.nutatut.com/ author/nupur/*

"Going back to the historical roots of mythological places can be a fascinating exercise for lovers of both mythology and history. Sayan Bhattacharya has done an eminent job in his book, *Ancient Cities of India*, bringing us both the history and mythology of some of the prominent cities mentioned in our great epics…

Bhattacharya brings alive the ancient cities as they existed during the times of the Mahabharata and the Ramayana. He narrates how the names of many of these cities underwent evolution as time passed.

Bhattacharya has taken much care to bring available historical evidences wherever required. The book can be good reference material for those who genuinely wish to know the history of the cities mentioned in India's great epics…"

"The present book 'Ancient Cities' penned by Sayan Bhattacharya covers cities of India and world. Author Sayan here comprehensively, yet incisively, studies the rise, growth and fall of republics of ancient cities. He has also dwelt upon the rise and expansion of kingdoms and growth and decline of towns, cities and various urban centres in different parts of the Indian subcontinent at length. It delves deep into modes of expansion of territories, factors leading to urbanisation and urbanisation patterns, and town planning. It presents a picturesque description of the urban centres of North India and more and pays special attention to dates related to founding of republics and cities, their extent, their functioning as administrative and religious centres, the problem of their identification and references to them in works, and their place in the wider framework of ancient Indian polity. The book will be useful to scholars and students interested in the study of ancient cities and urban history. Of all the ancient cities mentioned in this book some of my personal favorite are – Bairat, Hastinapur, Lahore, Multan and Varanasi.

There is lot more in the book apart from these 5 ancient cities I have mentioned. This is one of the best books you can read and re-read on Ancient Cities. A lot of research has been done by the author, but still lot more can be done. This book is the first step in acknowledging the true antiquity of our rich cultural history. This is an excellent, informative and well-written book about civilizations which had some points largely unknown. I highly recommend it to anyone interested history. This is an erudite and impressive work. There is a lot of dense information packed into this small volume. I was exposed to a tremendous amount of information about which I had no idea. Sayan, Congratulations for bringing out such an interesting book and I am glad that I have read it.

Content Rating: 5/5

- *Review Post dated 21 June 2018, by popular blogger and writer,* **Romila Chitturi,** *on her blog www. novemberschild.com*

Twitter bytes about *Ancient Cities of India*

"Fantastic writing… Brilliantly researched and very crisply written. I guess we have found our own William Dalrymple in you…"

"Sayan's in-depth research and informative stories are a treat to non-fiction readers…"

"Descriptive writing with minute detailing is this author's style…"

"Author Sayan's tireless research on ancient Indian cities brings life to the places as he presents those in his book…"

"Incredible posts... I devoured them crazily. This is one of my favourite genres and you made me so proud of our roots."

"Your posts are so detailed and so much facts. Liked the stories about the history…"

"Mighty impressed. Serious research and insight into Indian history. Kudos to you for writing this…"

"Wonderful read. You have traced the history from its origins right down to modern times in historical context. I love the way you include details and bring home the splendour of the cities during historical times…"

"Each time I read your posts I am enriched with a little more knowledge about history and mythology. As a lover of history, I am so happy for that. Thank you…"

"Ancient Cities of India is a perfect history read…"

Disclaimer

The information cited in this Book about the ancient cities mentioned therein has been compiled from the author's own study and reading of various books on Indian mythology, Indian history and validated sources found online on wiki, websites and journals related to the cities and the times about which the content has been written. No portion has been copied or claimed from any of these sources, except for the sections mentioned in 'quotes' for which the sources have also been mentioned.

The work and content of this Book may not be construed as a wholly authenticated version of mythology and/or history as it is merely a compilation of information from various sources and a re-telling of historical events as they have been recorded in time, done to the best of efforts by the author. Neither the author nor this Book does in any way intend to hurt, damage or counter any religious, patriotic or nationalist beliefs, and/or sentiments of any of its readers, communities or the public at large.

Any queries or comments regarding this Book and its contents may be directed to the author. All rights on the contents of this Book are reserved with the author.

****

A Note from the Author

That India has a rich historical and mythological heritage is not unknown but hidden in the folds of such mythology and history are cities which once sparkled with glory. We are aware about many such ancient cities of our country from the *Vedas, Puranas* and mythological legends. In later *Vedic* periods, accounts of historians and chroniclers from India, Greece, China and the Arabian region have given us legendary tales and information about many cities which were once imperial seats of power, home to many dynasties, steeped in religion, learning and culture, thus having etched their names in history forever.

My attempt in this Book has been to alphabetically showcase a selection of such ancient cities which have had an impactful existence in ancient India, but have either faded into insignificance later, or changed their character and name having fallen into the hands of other rulers, or with time and calamities have been erased from the face of the world. In my articles on these ancient cities I hope to share with my readers some of the lesser known stories about these cities and the role they had played in their times, while in the process also tracing the history of these cities down to the modern times wherever possible.

I hope my readers will enjoy this re-telling of history and the stories that come with it.

Thank you…

Sayan Bhattacharya

Contents

Ahichchhatra and Ajayameru

Ahichchhatra

Ahichchhatra, also known as *Ahi-kshetra*, was the capital of the *Uttar* (North) Panchala kingdom during the time of the Mahabharata. The city derives its name from the legend of an Ahir King, Adi Raja (Lord Vishnu) resting under the hooded canopy of the serpent Vasuki. In Sanskrit, the word Ahi means serpent and 'Chhatra' means an umbrella or canopy. Hence the place came to be called Ahichchatra. The 'Ahirs' were a tribe who worshipped the serpents, and belonged to the ancient 'Naga' group of people, and the region of Ahichchhatra was known as the 'kshetra' (region) of the Nagas.

During the time of the Mahabharata, Ahichchatra was a prosperous city ranging about 18 square miles and its adjacent region extended upto 40 hectares, thus making it one of the largest cities of its times. It was the second-most important city in the un-divided kingdom of Panchala, ruled by King Drupad.

We are aware of the friend-turned-foe relationship between Guru Dronacharya and King Drupad and legend has it that Guru Dronacharya sent his best pupil Arjun in arms, to 'teach a lesson' to his earlier friend King Drupad. Arjuna, executing the wishes of his master, captured King Drupad and brought him bound to Dronacharya. Drupad had earlier mocked the Guru saying that friendship could only happen between equals and while he was a King, Dronacharya was a mere poor Brahmin who had nothing. As King Drupad was captured by Arjuna and his kingdom annexed to Hastinapur, the kingdom was divided into two parts, Uttar (north) and Dakshin (south) Panchala and Uttar Panchala was given to Guru Dronacharya and Dakshin Panchala returned to King Drupad. Thus Dronacharya now became equal to King Drupad in the status of a King over Uttar Panchal.

The city of Kampilya continued to remain as the capital of South Panchala, while the prosperous city of Ahichchatra was made the new capital of North Panchala and was given to Guru Dronacharya by the aid of the Kurus of Hastinapur. However, as the Guru merely wanted to 'teach Drupad a lesson and demolish his pride', and had no real intentions of ruling over the kingdom as a King, Ahichchatra and north Panchala was given to Dronacharya's son Ashwathama who continued to rule the kingdom being subordinate to the rulers of Hastinapur.

The city of Ahichchatra flourished and continued to remain till the end of the Mahabharata war post which we do not find much mention of the city either in the mythological or historical texts. However, there are mentions of Jain temples and Buddhist stupas being erected in the region, which date back to the Gupta period of Indian history. Even Ahichchatra finds a singular mention in the accounts of Hieuen Tsang who said that the region had quite a few stupas and temples when he visited there around 630-640 AD.

The site of Ahichchatra was excavated in 1940-44 and much of the ruins were discovered in modern-day Ramnagar, a village located in Bareilly district of Uttar Pradesh.

****

Ajayameru

In the period 721 to 734 AD, there ruled a powerful King called Ajayaraja I in the line of the valiant Chahamana dynasty of the Rajputs. The Chahamanas are better known in history as the *Chauhans* and Ajayaraja I is said to be one of the first Kings in their dynasty. The Chauhans ruled from Shakambhari *(modern-day Sambhar)* in Rajputana. During the latter part of his reign, Ajayaraja I commissioned a fort to be built on top of a hill in his kingdom, in the Aravalli mountain range. Once the fort was built, he named it *'Taragarh'* – the Star Fort – given its magnificence and brilliant position on the top of the hitherto un-named hill. Gradually settlements began to form on the foothills and slopes leading up to the Taragarh fort.

His successor Ajayaraja II, chose to develop the region in the foothills of Taragarh, taking the opportunity of safety that the hill and the fort presented for the region, and gradually a city came up. The king called the city *'Ajayameru'* - the indestructible hill. [*Ajaya* meaning invincible and *meru* meaning hill]. Gradually with more of local and colloquial influence the city *Ajayameru* came to be called **'Ajmer'**, the name with which we know it today.

During the reign of Prithviraj Chauhan, the most valiant of the Chauhan Kings, the *Chahamana Empire* extended over majority of Rajputana and also included Delhi. Ajmer shone bright as the capital of this extensive empire. However, it was not before long that history handed down a fatal twist to Ajmer. Once Prithviraja Chauhan, fell in the battle with Muhammad Ghori in 1192, the new Islamic rulers of Hindustan wreaked havoc on all the kingdoms of Northern India, waging bloody wars. Muhammad Ghori's slave-general in Delhi, Qutbuddin Aibak, did not waste time in marching against Ajmer and for the first time in history, Ajmer's Taragarh fort was breached and the city captured.

Though after the death of Qutbuddin Aibak in 1210, the Chauhans had briefly recovered parts of their kingdom, but the respite was only short-lived as Aibak's son-in-law Iltutmish continued the sway of the Islamic rulers and gradually recaptured the territories once again. Iltutmish is also credited with enhancing the mosque hurriedly built by Aibak on the slopes of Taragarh hill in Ajmer, during his first campaign. The mosque and its extended precincts still stand today, famous as the *'Adhai din ka jhopra'* as it is said to have built hurriedly within two and a half days.

Ajmer, an important city in Rajasthan today, is also home to the famous Dargah Sharif - tomb of the Chisti founder of Sufi saints, *Khwaja Moinuddin Chisti*. Sufism was greatly promoted by the Mughals in India and like many other Sufi shrines, Ajmer too was well looked after by the *Mughal Badshahs*.

Bairat

The present city of Bairat is situated in the north Jaipur district of Rajasthan and lies about 50 kilometres north of Jaipur and 66 km west of Alwar. Built on a mound of ruins, modern-day Bairat appears a small place, but it has a history fascinating enough to woo a traveller to fancy a detour to visit the place. The mound of ruins on which Bairat lies today is more than three times the expanse of the present city and thus can be gauged the extent and prosperity of this city in its past.

The history of Bairat, traces back to the days of the Mahabharata, when it was called Viratnagar the capital of the Matsyadesa, and was founded by King Virat in whose kingdom the Pandavas had taken refuge in disguise during their thirteenth and final year of exile. The Mahabharata describes Viratnagar and the kingdom to be a prosperous place and a magnificent city, befitting the powerful ruler King Virat and his royal family.

In the later Vedic period, the Chedis ruled over Viratnagar and then the Mauryans. Inscriptions and relics of stupas and a rock-edict by Ashoka discovered among the ruins during excavation bear testimony that during the time of the Mauryan Empire, Viratnagar came under influence of Buddhism. The city also finds a mention in the travel accounts of Chinese pilgrim and Buddhist monk Hieuen

Tsang who visited in 634 AD and had written a description of the place, citing that it was mostly dominated by the Hindu Brahmin priests and their people while there were still evidences of eight Buddhist monasteries, though they were already in ruins at that time.

The next historical mention of Bairat is noticed during the time of Mahmud of Ghazni's attacks on India. Mahmud first attacked Bairat in 1009 when the Raja of the city submitted without any resistance. Mahmud sacked the city and looted its treasures, returning again in 1014 to continue his loot. However, this time the Hindus fought back but were defeated in a bloody battle and the city surrendered. As per historian Ferishta, there is however an ambiguity on the date and purpose of Mahmud's second attack on Bairat. Ferishta places the date at 1022, and says that the Sultan hearing that the people of Kairat and Nardin (Bairat and nearby town of Narayan) were still practising idol worship contrary to the faiths and beliefs of Islam, which Mahmud was known to have imposed on the kingdoms he conquered, resolved to forcibly compel them to the Mohammedan faith. Accordingly his general Amir Ali plundered the cities of Narayan and Bairat, indiscriminately killing Hindus and desecrating their shrines and looting the temples.

Some historians, based on later research, state that Mahmud's armies found some rock edicts in the Buddhist ruins near Narayan which suggested that the temple of Narayan had been built forty thousand years ago and that they may have mistaken the lion symbol of Ashoka as an image of idol worship, thus deciding to attack and kill the populace of the towns *en masse.*

The ancient city of Viratnagar was thus deserted for some centuries after the attacks of Mahmud and saw repopulation once again during the reign of the Mughal Emperor Akbar. Those were prosperous times and as Abul Fazal mentions in his Ain-i-Akbari, "the region of Bairat presented very profitable copper mines". The ancient city and the name of Viratnagar had disappeared by then, to be replaced by the more common lore of Bairat.

Modern-day Bairat stands at 50 kms away from Jaipur on the way to Delhi, and is mostly populated by the Gaur Brahmins and Agarwal baniyas. The fate of the once majestic capital of Viratnagar is now one reduced to insignificance.

Champapuri

References to Champapuri are found in both Ramayana and Mahabharata. However we can also find traces of this iconic ancient city in earlier mythology as well. The legend of churning of the ocean by the Devas and Asuras in search of the holy nectar of immortality is well known to any reader of Indian mythology. What many may not know though is that the venue of the event was in a place called Bhagdatpuram, which meant the 'city of luck'! Mount Mandar was used as the pivot for the churning and the benevolent snake god Vasuki offered himself as the rope for the process.

Mount Mandar, a 800 feet high granite hill still stands today at Bhagdatpuram, its sides bearing the indelible marks of the coils created by Vasuki's body acting as the rope during the churn. There are impressions of a lot of relics from the bygone ages on the hill. However, the venue Bhagdatpuram, across the centuries have gathered a colourful history.

In the epic Mahabharata, the region and city was referred to as part of the Anga kingdom and was gifted to Karna by the Kuru prince Duryodhana. Karna ruled the Anga kingdom from a magnificent capital named Champapuri which is said to be on the same locales of Bhagdatpuram. Later, the city of Malini was also gifted to Karna by Jarasandha and was included in the Anga kingdom.

In later Vedic period, the Anga kingdom flourished and the kings ruled from its capital Champa, until it was included as a part of the Mauryan Empire of Magadh. We find a handful of rock-edicts, inscriptions and caves with Ashoka's inscriptions that talk about the Buddhist influence in the place. Later, the Guptas, built Hindu temples and patronised the city during their reign. Dharmapala, the Buddhist king of Gauda (Bengal), in the post Gupta period, extended his sway over Champa and the Anga kingdom and the region saw flourish of the Mahayana Buddhism traditions and culture. Dharmapala is also credited with establishing the Vikramshila Mahavihara (university), a short distance away from Champa.

During the reign of King Harsha in Kannauj, the Anga kingdom came to be included in his empire as it was acceded to him in the battle with the Pala kings of Bengal. The entire eastern region flourished greatly under Harsha and was popularly called Anga-Banga-Kalinga (Eastern Bihar, Bengal and Odisha, in modern day geographic alignment). The famous Chinese monk and pilgrim Hieuen Tsang visited Champa in the 7th century and wrote about a large harbour situated at Champanagar (now known as Champanala) on the Ganges, which flowed through the western boundary of the city. Later excavations carried out in the 1970s, in the place, revealed relics of boats and coins even from the Middle and Far Eastern countries, which signify that Champa was an important centre for trade.

Following the Muslim conquest of the Indian heartland by Qutbuddin Aibak, Iltutmish and later the Khilji dynasty, the place gradually changed its character and came to be annexed by the Khilji generals of Bengal province. By then the ancient name of Champapuri had disappeared and the exact location of the city had also become blurred. The scattered settlements in and around the area came to be known as Bhagalpur, a name adopted from the mythological name of the city: Bhagdatpuram. Bhagalpur thus remained under the Muslim province of Bengal thereafter.

During the reign of Mughal Emperor Akbar, Bhagalpur was passed to the Delhi Empire when Akbar's forces conquered Bengal, and remained a part of it until it was given away to the East India Company in a grant by the Mughal Emperor Shah Alam II in 1765. Bhagalpur acted as a very important centre for trade and commerce in the Bengal Presidency during the British Raj.

Though the name Champapuri has long disappeared, the city still lives on, albeit in a different character and a successful city in the modern times. Bhagalpur, included in India's recent 'Smart City' development programme, has always lived up to maintain an appreciable balance of its heritage and tradition while surging ahead in modern development.

Dwarka

The mythical city of *Dvaraka*

No account of the ancient cities of India can be complete without the mention of its most sparkling and magnificent mythical city, the capital of Lord Krishna's empire, Dwarka. The city with its fantastic myths and rich history stakes a claim to pre-date the earliest settlements discovered on the Indian subcontinent and establishes its existence to almost nine thousand years ago.

Mythology has it that Dwarka was built by Lord Krishna on even an earlier sacred city called *Kusasthali*, established by the Aryans during the *Puranaic* age in Saurashtra. The rebuilding of the city after the settlement of the Yadavas who migrated from Mathura and the subsequent history is well cited in the *Mahabharata*, which remains the major source of information about the mythical Dwarka. It is said that Krishna left Mathura after fighting Jarasandha, the King of Magadha, and settled here. He reclaimed 12 *yojanas* of land (96 square kilometres) from the sea to recreate Dwarka.

Krishna named the city Dwarka (Sanskrit: *Dvaraka*) meaning 'the city of gates', where *Dvar* in Sanskrit means gate and *'ka'* is a reference to the multiple grand gates the city was known to have. Many believed it to be the *'gateway to heaven'* and visited Dwarka to attain salvation. The city was also known by other names like, *'Dvarika'*, and *'Dvaravati'*.

As described in the *Bhagavat Purana*, Dwarka was a city filled with sights and sounds of happiness: of birds and bees, of flowery gardens and parks, streams of water trickling along its well-lined channels. The roads, commercial streets and residential districts were well laid out and the city boasted of innumerable palaces which were furnished with sparkling jewels and grand curtains. Of these, the quarters of Lord Krishna and his queens were the most notable and opulent, which according to legend were constructed by the demi-god of architecture, Vishwakarma himself. Overall the city shone with such ornate structures, opulent mansions and glowing magnificence that it was often referred to as the *'city of gold'*.

Dwarka, though such a brilliant city and the capital of an equally worthy empire, was often fraught with risks of attacks from the demon kings. Notable among them was the *Asura* king *Salva*, who often plagued Krishna and had on one occasion, even destroyed parts of the glittering Dwarka with energy weapons shot from his super-fast flying craft, the description of which is also found in the *Mahabharata*. For the witnesses to that raging battle between Krishna and Salva over the skies of Dwarka, *"Salva's flying craft discharged weapons which flew like lightning strikes on the city of Dwarka."* However, Krishna was successful in turning the tide of the battle and saving his city.

Dwarka finds innumerable mention in the *Puranas*, texts like the *Harivamsa* and probably the maximum in the epic *Mahabharata*. The *Pandavas* visited Dwarka during their exile, and even after their successful campaign at the *Kurukshetra* war, Arjuna came back to Dwarka. But the most important reference to Dwarka found in the *Mahabharata* (in the *Mausala Parva*) is in the words of Arjuna, who loved the city very much and had returned to visit the place with his brothers before the *Pandavas* retired from the world. The lament in Arjuna's words on seeing the ornate city being submerged by the ocean is a fitting tribute to the mythical Dwarka, lost forever:

"The sea which had been beating against the shores, suddenly broke the boundary imposed on it by nature. The sea rushed into the city. It coursed through the streets of this beautiful city. The waters slowly covered up everything in the city. I saw the beautiful buildings and mansions being submerged one by one. In a matter of few moments it was all over. The sea had become placid as a lake. There was no trace left of the city... Dvaraka was just a name, just a memory."

The mythical *Dvaraka* was said to have been submerged in the ocean and thus destroyed, within a short span of Krishna leaving the earth. Mythology has it that Krishna's departure and the destruction of Dwarka at the hands of nature, heralded the advent of the *'kali yuga'* (the current time-cycle of the universe as per Hindu scriptures) around the time of 3102 BC.

In the period 1983 - 1990, the marine archaeological excavations conducted by the Indian Institute of Oceanography, yielded miraculous findings of ruins of a city ranging a distance of 9 Kms, submerged in the sea off the coast of the Bay of Cambay. Dr S S Rao, an eminent Indian archaeologist confirms, *"The available archaeological evidence from on-shore and off-shore excavations confirms the existence of a city-state with a couple of satellite towns dating back to the period of 1500 BC."* He considered it reasonable to conclude that this submerged city is the *Dvaraka*, as described in the *Mahabharata*.

Dwarka in later history

The current location of Dwarka is also based on a city founded by Krishna near the mouth of the River Gomti. In about 200 AD, the *Mahakshatriya* Rudradama defeated the King of Dwarka, Vasudev II and established his rule. He embraced *Vaishnava* religion and worshipped Krishna in Dwarka. Later, his successor, Vajranabha built a small temple structure and deified an idol of Krishna in it. This was later on accentuated and built on a grander scale into the *Dwarakadheesh Temple* with Krishna as the supreme deity. *Vaishnava Hinduism* as a religious sect flourished for the next few centuries across the country and during 686 and 717 AD, *Adi Shankaracharya* brought Dwaraka into the folds of the *'Char Dhaam'* (the four religious seats) of Hinduism, thus catapulting Dwarka as a prominent religious pilgrim centre for the Hindus entrenching the *Dwarakadheesh Temple* at its heart.

Both Dwarka and its grand temple suffered similar fates in the ensuing centuries, being plundered repeatedly at the hands of the Muslim invaders: in 1241 by Mohammed Shah and in 1473 by Mahmud Begada, the Sultan of Gujarat when the province was completely conquered and wrested by the Muslim rulers. Such skirmishes went on till the time of the British Raj and the *Dwarakadheesh Temple* was rebuilt and repaired many times after repeated invasions, loots and destructions.

The city of Dwarka, as it stands today, bears a stoic history of proudly living its ancient lineage and remains a sparkling jewel in the cultural heritage of our country.

Ek-Chakra-Nagri

*D*oing *the research for this quaint town of ancient
Aryavarta has been such a surprising journey. At the outset,
the name came across striking an intrigue and then multiple
modern locations of today staked their claim to fame to be
the modern avatar of the mythological Ek-Chakra-Nagari.
However, after much research and logical eliminations, I
have gone ahead with the most plausible one.*

The mythological connection

Ek-Chakra-Nagari finds its first mention in the
Mahabharata as a small township on the banks of the
Yamuna in the Doab region, where the Pandava brothers
and their mother Kunti arrive, shortly after escaping the
near-fatal *lakshagriha* episode. It is in this village that
the Pandavas come to know about the King of the region
holding a grand *swayamvara* ceremony for his daughter, at
his capital Kampilya.

From the description and classification of kingdoms in
Aryavarta during the *Mahabharata* times, Kampilya was
the capital of the South Panchala kingdom, ruled over by
King Drupad, someone well known to the Pandava brothers
for reasons not so pleasant. His daughter for whom the
swayamvara was being organised was the most beautiful
princess Panchali (*a.k.a* Draupadi).

The Pandavas were dressed as wandering Brahmins and that is how they acquainted with the Brahmins of *Ek-Chakra-Nagari*, who very excitedly told them about the magnificent ceremony and the *swayamvara* scheduled in Kampilya. The ensuing legend is quite well known to all, where the Pandava brothers reached the swayamvara in the guise of Brahmins along with the group of the *Ek-Chakra-Nagari* Brahmins, who had merely come in the hope of obtaining some worthy gifts and benefits completely unaware of their accompanying guests, and how Arjuna then won the hand of Panchali by display of his excellent archery skills.

Apart from being famous for guiding the Pandavas to Draupadi's *swayamvara*, *Ek-Chakra-Nagari* is also well known in *Mahabharata* for yet another important reason. It is the place where Bhima had slayed the cannibal-demon *Bakasur* and saved the village folk from his oppression.

Later history

As the centuries passed and time moved into the later Vedic periods, the town of *Ek-Chakra-Nagari* remained insignificant and the only major activity that occurred in the area was brick building. Gradually, the name *Ek-Chakra-Nagari* was lost with disuse and gave way to a new name: *'Etawah'*, which was derived from the existence of many brick kilns in the area. We still know this city as 'Etawah', however it is quite a flourishing town in Uttar Pradesh today.

Etawah flourished as a centre for trade and commerce during the Gupta period and later under the *Pratiharas* who ruled over the area from their capital Kannauj. Though it did not grow into an important town-centre or city during the 6th and 7th centuries when the kingdom rose to its height of prosperity under kings like *Mihir Bhoja* and *Harshavardhan,* Etawah was generally referred to as an important crossing town on the banks of the Yamuna and was visited enroute by travellers. In the words of a historian contemporary of the *Pratihara* king *Mihir Bhoja*, *"the region of Etawah is prosperous, safe from thieves and rich in natural resources."*

With the fall of Delhi and Kannauj in 1193, the two major power centres of Hindustan at that time, at the hands of *Sultan Sihabuddin Muhammad Ghori*, Etawah too was involved in the initial skirmishes between the independent Hindu kings and the invading Muslim armies under *Ghori* and *Qutbuddin Aibak*. Finally, along with most of the other Hindu kingdoms which passed on to the hands of the Turkic Muslim rulers, by 1215, Etawah too was annexed by the Muslim powers under *Iltutmish*. The next few centuries saw immense conflicts between the Muslim rulers of Hindustan with the *Suris*, *Lodhis* and *Shahs* fighting for supremacy over the territories. Then came the Mughals and Etawah fell in the path of *Babur* and later *Humayun* as they tried to advance deeper into the Ganga-Yamuna doab region. Humayun is said to have killed Qutb Khan, the ruler of Etawah at that time and annexed the place.

The city saw many battles and scars, forts built, captured, destroyed and rebuilt, and even the Marathas from the west had also claimed rule at Etawah for couple of occasions. In 1774, Etawah was made a part of the *Province of Awadh*, ruled over by Shuja-ud-daula, the *Nawab of Oudh*. However, in 1801, the reigning Nawab, Saadat Ali Khan ceded Etawah and the neighbouring areas to the British and the city was yet again passed from one era of rulers to another.

We find the next significant mention of Etawah in history during the 1857 Mutiny against the British Raj. Following the outbreak of the Mutiny in the sepoy ranks at Meerut on 11th May, the news spread like wildfire and soon many battalions and regiments stationed in different centres across North India joined the rebellion against their English masters. As Gwalior, Agra, Delhi, Jhansi, Farukhhabad and other nearby centres blew up in rebellion, Etawah was also embroiled in the fire of mutiny against the British. However, as by December of that year, most of the rebellion bursts had being quelled, in Etawah too, the mutineers were squashed and executed by the British armies and the city recaptured by them without much effort.

Post-independence, Etawah has returned to be a quiet and peaceful city with the promise of growth and development.

Contrary to many ancient cities of India, Etawah may just have had a singular shot at its mythological grandeur, but the subsequent history of the city has not been any less fascinating to learn about.

Fatehpur

As the Slave Dynasty commenced the Islamic rule in India around 1200 AD, under Qutbuddin Aibak, the slave general of Muhammad Ghori, and later Sultan Iltutmish, the immediate consolidation of their empire happened through wars and annexations of the different kingdoms present in Hindustan at that time. After having subdued the imperial city of Kannauj, Iltutmish's son Nasiruddin Mahmud had turned his forces to a nearby town of *Asani (also known as Asi in the earlier Sanskrit texts).*

The town of Asani, though not of major importance in the political scenario of Hindustan, was famous for its impregnable fortress which armies of the invaders had earlier repeatedly failed to breach. The fortress had been built by the ruling *Chedi* kings to protect the town from the attacks of the other warring kingdoms of north India. The location of Asani is identified to be between Allahabad and Kanpur, being about 117 kms from the former and 75 kms from the latter.

The Vedic Era connection

The city of Asani traced its origins to the Vedic era and its neighbouring town *Bhitaura* was known to have been the seat of the legendary sage *Bhrigu*, who is revered as one of the *Saptarshis*. The region of Asani was a part of the *Vatsa* kingdom in the Vedic era, ruled over by the *Vatsa* kings who were a branch of the *Kuru* dynasty of *Hastinapur* (ref. *Mahabharata*). The *Vatsas* ruled from their capital *Kaushambi,* a city known to have been found by the Lunar king *Kusa. [Kaushambi has been identified with Prayag of the later medieval period and modern day Allahabad.]*

The *Vatsya* kingdom was one of the 16 *Mahajanapadas* (great kingdoms) of *Aryavarta* in the Vedic period and from that time itself Asani was a town situated near their eastern border, which they shared with another mighty kingdom *Madhyadesha.*

In the later Vedic periods and also during the Maurya and Gupta regimes, Asani experienced the rise of Buddhism and later Brahminical Hinduism as its religious and cultural vein. Sanskrit was the main language of the region. The later excavations in the region of Asani and Bhitaura have revealed findings and inscriptions which validate the emphatic influence of Buddhism and Hinduism in the area. The famous Chinese pilgrim and Buddhist monk, Hieuen Tsang is also said to have visited Asani in 630 AD during his travels in the region. Further, the archaeological excavations have validated the time period of the Asani fortress through the remnants of the bricks which were used in its construction.

Later history

Nasiruddin Mahmud, Iltutmish's son is credited with the

conquest of Asani as he successfully broke through the once invincible fort of the town and captured the city, around 1226. Such was the euphoria of this victory and for finally breaching the un-conquerable Asani fortress, that the Delhi Sultan joyously named the city **'Fatehpur'** (*Fateh* meaning victory). Thereafter the administration and governance of the region passed on to the Turkic generals and it became part of the Delhi Sultanate. The city lost its original name of Asani and has been since referred to as Fatehpur.

As centuries rolled on and with time new Sultans occupied the *'takht-e-Dilli'* (throne of Delhi), Fatehpur remained insignificant in its place as a quiet town. In 1561, Emperor Humayun invaded the nearby Jaunpur state, the tremors of which were felt in Fatehpur. But in 1659, the city saw a bloody war on its turf when Aurangzeb fought a fierce battle with his brother prince Shah Shuja, (who was the governor of Bengal at that time) at Fatehpur. In the later Mughal period when the powers of the Mughal Emperors at Delhi started waning, Fatehpur changed hands between the rulers of Jaunpur, Kannauj and Delhi.

During the British Raj, in 1801, Fatehpur and the nearby region was ceded to the East India Company and was soon made a sub-division and in 1826 the district headquarters. Fatehpur made its mark in the Indian independence movement when during the outbreak of the 1857 Mutiny, a group of English officers were allegedly attacked and hanged on trees by mutineers storming the city.

Today Fatehpur stands as an upcoming city, one among the

thirty-four cities benefitted by the grants from the *Grants Fund Programme of the Government of India*, and a notable station on the Kanpur-Allahabad rail route.

[Note: The city Fatehpur described above is not to be confused with Fatehpur-Sikri situated near Agra.]

Girivraja

The mythical connection

Girivraja was an ancient city with its origins clearly defined in Indian mythology. In the *Valmiki Ramayan, Bal-khand, Sargas 2 and 31 to 33*, while roaming in exile, Lord Ram asks Rishi Vishwamitra about the place where they were presently visiting. Rishi Vishwamitra replies that they were at a city called Girivraja, near the banks of the Son River, and goes on to relate how the city came into existence.

In the *Somavansha* (Lunar dynasty) line of kings, even much before the Ramayana period, in *Aryavarta* there lived a popular king called *Kusa*, who directed his four sons, Kushamba, Kushanabha, Asurtaraja and Vasu each to build a city in his kingdom and govern. Kushamba built the city *Kaushambi* which was named after him, Kushanabha built *Mahodaya* and Asurtaraja built *Dharmaranya* while the youngest son Vasu built *Girivraja* near the Son River. As the location of the city was surrounded by hills and was a verdant landscape, he called it '*Girivraja*' - the place of the hills.

Girivraja flourished under Vasu's descendant Brihadratha and was the capital of his kingdom Magadha. Girivraja again finds mention in the Mahabharata as the resplendent imperial city of the King of Magadha, Jarasandha. In fact, during the time of the Mahabharata, Magadh is often referred to as the most powerful kingdom in Aryavarta, even stronger than the territories ruled over by the *Kurus* and the *Panchals*. The enmity between Krishna and Jarasandha is almost a folk-lore and it is said that Jarasandha of Magadh had attacked Krishna's city Mathura eighteen times, until finally the *Yadavas* decided to migrate from there and set up their new kingdom in Dwarka.

Jarasandha allied with Duryodhana and supported his claim to the Hastinapur throne. As per popular folk-lore, Krishna, Arjuna and Bhima are said to have entered Jarasandha's capital Girivraja in disguise and in an ensuing wrestling combat Bhima killed Jarasandha in an unfair contest. Later the Pandava brothers placed Jarasandha's son on the throne of Girivraja and he died fighting for the Pandavas in the Kurukshetra war.

Girivraja during the time of Lord Buddha

During the time of the Buddha (450 BC), Magadha was a flourishing kingdom under King Bimbisara, who ruled from Girivraja. However, by that time, the name of the city had been changed from Girivraja to **Rajagriha** (meaning *'house of the royals'*). Rajagriha was a decorated city and the grandeur was one to behold. Gautama Siddhartha, the heir prince of the *Lichchavi* kingdom (north of Magadh and modern day Nepal) came wandering to Magadh, having visited many other kingdoms. It was in the kingdom of Magadh, at a site near Gaya that Siddhartha attained enlightenment (the site famously known as Bodh Gaya) and became the Buddha. King Bimbisara was among the countless who were influenced by the Buddha and started propagating the new religion.

However, Bimbisara's son Ajatashatru turned out to be a cruel and ruthless monarch. He usurped the throne from his father and imprisoned him, keeping him in captivity in Rajagriha till the end of his life. In a significant development, Ajatashatru moved the capital of Magadh from Rajagriha to the newly found city of Pataliputra (modern day Patna). It was destined for Pataliputra to rise and shine for generations ahead to be the imperial and glorious capital of, first, the Magadh kingdom and then the Mauryan Empire, while Rajagriha continued to play the second fiddle.

A religious and cultural learning centre

Rajagriha may have had lost the race in imperial glory with the capital being shifted to Pataliputra, but the city soon became an important and popular seat of religious-cultural learning under the Mauryas. In the 5th Century BC, the *Nalanda Mahavihara* (university) was established in its vicinity and its flourish saw the advent of new methods of learning. Religious discourses across classical Hinduism, Buddhism and Jainism prevailed in the university and the medium of language was primarily Sanskrit, Pali and Prakrit. Emperor Ashoka was one of its principal patrons.

With the waning of the erstwhile *Takshashila mahavihara* in the North-western part of India at that time, Nalanda continued to attract scholars from all over *Aryavarta* and also from other countries. Later *Vikramshila* and *Tamralipta mahaviharas* were set up on the same model. After the Mauryas, *Nalanda mahavihara* flourished under the patronage of the Gupta Kings in the 5th and 6th Centuries AD and later under King Harsha of Kannauj. We get excellent references and information about Rajagriha and Nalanda from the accounts of the Chinese monks *Hieuen Tsang* and *Fa Hien,* both of whom had stayed and studied there.

The *Nalanda mahavihara* continued to function till about 1200 AD, when it was completely destroyed in the attacks by the invading Muslim armies of the Slave Dynasty of Qutbuddin Aibak, during the invasion of Bengal led by a Turkic general Bakhtiyar Khilji. Rajagriha and Nalanda were both ransacked, looted and damaged to a large extent during the battles raged by Khilji in the region. While Nalanda was abandoned and deserted soon after the annexation of the region by the Delhi Sultanate, Rajagriha lived on as a town but was relegated into insignificance.

Modern times

It was sometime during the rule of the different Turkic and Islamic rulers after 1300 AD, that the name of the city was adapted to the more colloquial **Rajgir**, from the erstwhile Rajagriha. Even during the British Raj, Rajgir was an important city of the Bihar-Bengal province and was well populated.

Today, Rajgir stands as an important centre on the religious circuit for Hindus, Buddhists and Jains alike and is also a popular tourist destination in Bihar. The *Nalanda mahavihara* ruins have also been excavated by the Archaeological Society of India and are preserved as testimony to its once glorious heritage.

Hastinapur

Hastinapur is certainly not an unfamiliar name to a reader of Indian mythology, being described as the glittering, glorious and powerful capital of the Kaurava clan in the epic Mahabharata. However, the first references to the location of Hastinapur comes as the capital of Emperor Bharata, the mythical king and ruler of the *Chandravanshi* (lunar dynasty) lineage from whom our country derives its name *'Bharatvarsha'* or *'Bharat'*.

pre-Mahabharata mythology and the origins of Hastinapur

Before we trace the origins of Hastinapur, for better understanding of the context, let us briefly understand the *Chandravanshi* lineage of kings, wherefrom the Kuru clan emerged.

The *Chandravanshi* (Lunar dynasty) commenced with Pururava, who was the son of Budh and Ila (daughter of Manu) and came down through his eldest son Ayu. The fourth King in this lineage was **Puru,** younger son of King Yayati *(a.k.a Jajati)* who pleased his father by taking on his old age upon himself and was in return blessed with the privilege of carrying forward the royal lineage of the Lunar dynasty, despite being the younger son. It is in the line of Puru, that the *Kauravas* and *Pandavas* descend *(jointly* *called the Pauravas after Puru's name),* while the *Yadavas* (Lord Krishna's lineage) descend from King Yayati's elder son, Yadu (thus Krishna's lineage is called the *Yadu-vansha*).

King **Bharata** is the sixteenth in the lineage from Puru and was said to have ruled over the region between the Ganga and Yamuna Rivers. Evidences from the *Mahabharata* as well as different *Puranas* state that at that time Bharata's capital was located on the earlier course of the Ganga River *(now known as Ban-Ganga or Budhi-Ganga, as the river had moved its course over time).* The location was approximately identified as forty miles south of Hardwar, where the Ganga breaks through the Sivalik Mountains and enters the plains of India. The *Puranas* also describe River Ganga near Bharata's capital city to be *"a mighty stream, rolling its masses of waters gushing down from the Himalyan glaciers, and joined by many auxiliary streams, descending on the plains with such a force that often brings destruction in its path…"*

However, it is important to note that though this city was the capital of King Bharata's empire, it had not yet acquired the name of Hastinapur at that time. It was four royal generations after Bharata that his descendant King **Hasti** accentuated the capital and built a royal city on it: one that was equally powerful and fortified as it was opulent and ornate. The imperial emblem adopted for the dynasty was the Elephant which signified might and grace, as also being aligned to the King's name. *Hasti* in *Sanskrit* meant 'Elephant' and therefore the city which King Hasti founded started to be known as *'Hastinapuram'* (or 'The Elephant City' as *'puram'* in *Sanskrit* meant city). Later the place came to be popularly known and called as **Hastinapur.**

After King Hasti, the next most powerful and famous king to rule the Paurava kingdom was **Kuru,** who ascended the throne at Hastinapur four royal generations after Hasti. The Paurava dynasty thereafter has been referred to as Kuru's dynasty and lineage, as Kuru is said to be the mightiest and the most illustrious king in the lineage. His kingdom was called the *Kuru rashtra* and his clan or descendants the *Kauravas.* It was only in the age of the Mahabharata that the Pandava line emerged from the Kaurava dynasty and was named after King Pandu.

Hastinapur in the times of Mahabharata

The story of Mahabharata primarily begins with King **Shantanu**, who is the thirteenth in the royal lineage and ascendency to the Hastinapur throne, after Kuru. King Shantanu's eldest son **Devavrat** (better known as *Bheeshma*) gave up his claim to the Hastinapur throne in favour of his half-brothers **Vichitravirya** and **Chitrangad** and vowed to forever protect the throne and the kingdom of Hastinapur. It is from this line of the Kuru kings that we have the later heroes of the Mahabharat, King **Dhritarashtra**, King **Pandu** and their respective descendants who called themselves the *Kauravas* and *Pandavas* respectively.

At the time of the Mahabharata era, Hastinapur was undoubtedly the most powerful and opulent city in entire *Aryavarta* and the *Kuru* kingdom was the most extensive. Led by Devavrat, a proficient warrior and leader par-excellence, most of the neighbouring kingdoms across North India were subjugated to the power of the *Kaurava*

King and owed their allegiance to Hastinapur. However, not all kingdoms were brought under subjugation by war by the *Kauravas,* but friendly ties and matrimonial alliances as well. The legends of the abduction of the princesses of *Kashi* (Benaras), Amba, Ambika and Ambalika by Devavrat and the subsequent marriage of Ambika and Ambalika to Vichitra Virya and Chitrangad; the marriage of the blind Dhritarashtra to Gandhari, the princess of the north-west kingdom of *Gandhara*; or the marriage of Kunti, adopted daughter of King Kunti-Bhoja in the *Yaduvanshi* line of the *Bhoja* kingdom in far west, are popular and well known in the *Mahabharata* and its related stories.

It is also mentioned in the *Mahabharata* and the *Puranas* that though many kings desired to rule over a grand and wealthy city like Hastinapur, no king in *Aryavarta* had the might to rage war against the Kauravas; and that the destruction of the *Kauravas* was brought about by their own feud and internal hostilities, is again well established.

The decline of Hastinapur and its destruction

Many have often thought that the imperial capital of the *Kauravas,* Hastinapur, was destroyed in the *Mahabharata* war as all the *Kauravas* were killed and the clan ended. However, such is not the case as Hastinapur lived on for at least thirteen more generations before it was destroyed. The lineage left behind by Arjuna, however continued for twenty seven more royal generations after the Pandavas, though they were called the *Kuru-vansh* (lineage) kings once again (and not the *Pandavas*).

At the end of the *Mahabharata* war at Kurukshetra, with the *Kaurava* clan being erased and Hastinapur being won over by the *Pandavas*, the eldest *Pandava* **Yudhisthir** ascended the throne at Hastinapur with queen Draupadi. While they had ensured that the *Kaurava* clan was completely decimated in the war, the *Kauravas* had also left no stone unturned in meting out the same treatment to the *Pandavas*. All their sons had been killed in the war and the only one left in the lineage was the un-born Parikshit, grandson of Arjuna, who was ensconced safely in his mother Uttara's womb. Legend has it that after the *Kaurava* princes and stalwarts had trapped and killed Arjuna's son Abhimanyu in the fatal *'chakravyuh'*, Duryodhan had wanted to even kill the un-born Parikshit in his mother's womb, but Yudhisthir had miraculously protected and saved him.

So when the dejected *Pandavas* decided to retire from the world, which was soon after Krishna's departure and the advent of *Kali Yuga*, they placed their only heir to the lineage, young **Parikshit,** on the throne of Hastinapur and departed from the kingdom towards the Himalayas.

[The Mahabharata era was towards the end of Dwapar Yuga which ended with the destruction of majority of Aryavarta at the Kurukshetra war. The time for this is estimated to be 3102 BC.]

The first two kings of Hastinapur during the immediate Kaliyuga, were of notable fame: Parikshit, who worked towards consolidation of the broken empire and rebuilding Hastinapur to a large extent; and his son **Janmejaya** who continued the work started by his father. It is also said that while wandering in the north-west regions of *Aryavarta*, King Janmejaya met sage Vaisampayan (son of the great sage Ved Vyas) at the location of Taxila *(present day north Pakistan),* who narrated to him the detailed story of his ancestors, which Janmejaya later recorded with the sage's permission. This is said to be one of the first written sources of the epic *Mahabharata.* However, the later kings of Hastinapur failed to hold on to their empire or to the might and influence of Hastinapur and gradually the kingdom and its capital fell in its significance.

It was during the reign of King **Nichakshu**, estimated around 900 BC, that a great deluge hit Hastinapur as the Ganga suddenly swelled and rose in mighty force. The ancient texts, *Matsya* and *Vayu Puranas*, describe this deluge lashing upon Hastinapur as *"swirling water columns of great force, risen to the perpendicular height of thirty feet bore away all within its sweep, thus lying Hastinapur to its ruin."* Post the deluge, the Ganga River moved its course away to its present location and left the city of Hastinapur completely submerged in silt and mud up to the height of a few storeys. Such was the destruction of this once grand and imperial city that the place was deserted and was not lived in by people for next few centuries. Later excavations and the inspection of the soil in Hastinapur region validate the great flood that is attributed to the destruction of the mythological city of Hastinapur.

The Kuru king Nichakshu left the place with his surviving people and moved his kingdom to **Kaushambi**, located 50 kms from modern day Allahabad. The Kuru lineage set up their new kingdom and continued to rule from Kaushambi for another fourteen generations, till they were decimated in territorial war during the later Vedic period, at the time of Kshemaka the last Kuru ruler. Mythology estimates that the time-period from Parikshit to the end of the Kuru line is 1050 years.

Resurgence of Hastinapur

It was almost towards the end of the later Vedic period that the region of Hastinapur started getting populated again. However, the place remained insignificant and its lost glory was never revived again. In later eras, some temples and structures were built in remembrance of the Mahabharata history and its heroes in the region and it became a centre for Hindus to visit and reminiscence the mythological legend. Samrat Samprati, the grandson of Asoka is believed to have built quite a few temples in this region, but those had later fallen into ruin or have been destroyed.

During the onset of the *Mughal Empire* in India, Hastinapur was invaded by Babur. During the British Raj period, the region of Hastinapur was ruled over by the local *Gujjar* king Raja Nain Singh Nagar, who has been credited with the efforts of restoration of some of the ancient temples.

Hastinapur today, though stands as a small town and *'nagar panchayat'* in the Meerut district of Uttar Pradesh, still reminds us of its revered history and heritage of the Mahabharata era, and is one of the few ancient places in India which can be traced back to pre-mythological times.

Indraprastha

Indraprastha is yet another ancient city of the mythological times which is famous for its pomp and grandeur. The origins of Indraprastha are described in the epic Mahabharata in the *'Khandav-dahan parva',* and the city is stated as the magnificent capital of the Pandavas and an important part of the *Kuru* kingdom.

The legend of Indraprastha

When the Pandavas returned to Hastinapur after marrying Draupadi, the elders of the Kuru family, Bheeshma, Dhritarashtra and Dronacharya offered to divide the kingdom into two and give one half of it to the Pandavas where they could set up their capital and rule, the other half including Hastinapur, to be ruled over by Kauravas. Duryodhana had to abide by the proposal, albeit grudgingly. The Pandava brothers accepted the proposal and went ahead to form their kingdom.

The Pandava share of the kingdom included a large forest called *Khandav-van* on the banks of the Yamuna River. It was a dense dark forest inhabited by demons and *nagas* (snakes) who constantly indulged in *'adharma'* (unjust) and illegal practices. They had made the *Khandav-van* an infamous place and though there were animals and birds galore in the forest, no one thought of the place with any positivity. While Krishna and Arjuna were searching for a suitable place to build their capital, Krishna suggested to Arjuna to burn down the *Khandav-van* and create their capital in that place. Accordingly, they sought the help of Agni who set fire to the expansive forest and devoured *Khandav-van* completely.

A more grounded mythological tale says that while *Khandav-van* was burning in the raging fire and all its nether-world inhabitants were dying in it, two people emerged from the fire and begged Arjuna to spare their lives. One was the last living King of the Indra tribes, who had been banished from Hastinapur and was living in exile, while the other was the demon architect Mayasura.

An alternate mythological version cites that the Indra tribe were the representatives of Lord Indra on earth and carried his god-like qualities. Also, the last Indra king had been chosen by *Rishi Ved Vyas* to impregnate queen Kunti during the birth of the Pandavas, as per the *Niyog pratha* followed at the time. The son born to Kunti from the last Indra king was Arjuna, who possessed similar divine qualities like Lord Indra. The reason for banishment of the last Indra King was due to the reason of the *Niyog pratha:* that he must not ever return to Hastinapur or appear in front of anyone from the Kuru royal family till he lived.

Mayasura, on the other hand, was an *Asura* but from the line of the divinely skilled architects, who had once been the pupil of Vishwakarma himself. Mayasura's ancestors who were expertly skilled in divine architecture were known to have built the *'Swarna-Lanka'* (the golden city of Lanka) for

Ravana in the *Treta Yuga*. But they had all been killed during the later wars waged against the *Asuras,* and Mayasura was the last of their line.

As Agni burned down the entire *Khandav-van* and the ground cleared, Mayasura built Indraprastha at the site, one of the most magnificent cities ever seen till that time. Mayasura was so grateful to Arjuna for having saved his life, that he delivered his best creation ever in building an opulent and ornate capital city for the Pandavas. Folklore says that at the completion of Indraprastha, Lord Vishwakarma himself was so pleased with the work of his disciple that he blessed Mayasura saying that the dazzling city he has created will live forever.

As the Indra king congratulated him on his new city, Arjuna said that he would like to name the city Indraprastha after his Indra father, as it was the place where the Indra king had been banished and had stayed in exile hiding in the *Khandav-van*, and it was also his way of paying tribute to the Indra tribe. The old man was very touched with the gesture of Arjuna and blessed him wholeheartedly.

[Traditional mythological texts, including the Mahabharata says that the city has been named so as it resembled the heavenly abode of Lord Indra in its grandeur and opulence.]

Indraprastha in the Mahabharata times

Apart from the story of its origins in the Mahabharata era, Indraprastha features for few more important events and references in the epic. The inauguration of Indraprastha was a grandiloquent affair and all the invited kings and guests remained awestruck and surprised with its magnificence. They showered praises and eloquent epithets describing the city and its grandeur which no one had hitherto seen, even the pomp of Hastinapur seemed to pale against it.

The jewel in the crown for Indraprastha was a jaded crystal palace specially built for the Pandavas by Mayasura. As per the works of Buitenen, the palace is described to have *"solid golden pillars... Radiant and divine, it had superb colour like the fire, or the sun, or the moon. Challenging as it were with its splendour, the luminous splendour of the moon, it shone divinely forth, as though on fire, with divine effulgence. It stood covering the sky like a mountain or monsoon cloud, long, wide, smooth, faultless, and dispelled fatigue. Made with the best materials, garlanded with gem-encrusted walls, filled with precious stones and treasures, it was built well by the Visvakarman. Neither the Sudharma hall of Krishna, nor the palace of Brahma possessed the matchless beauty that Maya imparted to it."*

It was in the backdrop of this extravagant Pandava capital that two quiet incidents occurred. Mayasura had built a special palace in Indraprastha called the Mayasabha (the gallery of illusions). It was exquisite yet illusory to the eye, and it was one such illusion at the Mayasabha that Duryodhana mistook a water-pool to be a marble platform and accidentally fell into, much to his embarrassment as many including the ladies of the house laughed on his *faux paus*. The enraged Duryodhana stormed out of Indraprastha after this incident burning in humiliation, vowing to punish the Pandavas for it in retribution.

The other incident, as mentioned in some alternate versions of mythology, occurred on the morning of the inauguration. At the centre of Indraprastha, Mayasura had built a large Shiva temple where the first pujas would be conducted as soon as the royal procession reached the temple. However, as the royal procession carrying Yudhisthir, Draupadi, Kunti and the Kaurava royal family from Hastinapur entered the city, Mayasura observed that the Ganesha idol at the first platform of the temple had developed a crack in it. He immediately asked Arjuna for some time so that he could repair the idol, as it was mandatory to first worship Ganesha and then proceed to the main pujas, and a damaged idol could not be worshipped. However, Arjuna disagreed saying that there was no time for any repairs and insulted Mayasura for not doing the job properly. Mayasura started to argue with him, citing that the idol may have been broken while it was being transported.

Further, Krishna spotted the Indra king present among the crowd who had thronged the streets waiting for the royal procession. The enraged Arjuna immediately ordered his guards to capture both the Indra King and Mayasura and send them out of Indraprastha. The guards followed their orders and immediately despatched both of them to the opposite bank of the Yamuna River. The worship rituals commenced and went on without the *Ganesha-pujas* and the entire inauguration event of Indraprastha carried on amidst great fanfare, while Mayasura and the Indra king watched dejectedly from the distance across the Yamuna River.

By the time the sun went down that day, Indraprastha stood glowing in its lamp lights glittering and presenting a golden and heavenly ambience. Mayasura could not hold his anger anymore at the ill-treatment meted out to him by Arjuna and seeing his own creation dazzling in front of his eyes, he cursed the city in rage: *"May this city be cursed and never be a safe place for its inhabitants for all its time to come!"*

Indraprastha – post Mahabharata to modern

At the end of the Kurukshetra war, the victorious Pandavas reigned from Hastinapur where King Yudhisthir ascended the throne. Arjuna held control over Indraprastha with Yuyutsa (the only Kaurava son of Dhritarashtra who had joined the Pandavas before the war) and the minor Vrishaketu (Karna's 9th son and his only heir who had survived the war). Arjuna had promised the dying Karna that he would take care of his minor son Vrishaketu and would raise him to be a proficient warrior and give Indraprastha to him when he attained the age fit to be a ruler.

The Pandavas ruled for a good thirty six years before they renounced the worldly life and retired to the heavens. During this period both Hastinapur and Indraprastha were under their reign and control. As the Pandavas departed, they placed Parikshit (Arjuna's minor grandson) on the throne of Hastinapur and Vrishaketu (Karna's son) on that of Indraprastha.

The story of Indraprastha from hereafter to the modern times is blurred as there has been no recorded account of how the city went into decline. However, some Puranas and ancient texts validate the existence of Indraprastha, in that the Kauravas and Pandavas fought each other over five *'prasthas'* (plains or places) later known in local as *'pats'*: Panipat, Sonepat, Baghpat, Tilpat and Indrapat. There is a strong belief that *Indrapat* refers to *Indraprastha*. Further, we have historial evidence of a village called *'Indrapat'* located in the Purana Qila area *(between Purana Qila and Humayun's tomb)* of Delhi, being in existence till 1913 post which it was demolished by the British. It is also believed that the Mughals constructed the Purana Qila (which was accentuated by Sher Shah) on the mounds or ruins of mythical Indraprastha.

The mythological references and description of its locations, followed by the references in later ancient texts like the *Puranas* and the polished grey ware pottery findings in the excavations conducted in the Purana Qila area of Delhi, all point towards the conclusion that the magnificent and mythological Indraprastha may well be called the ancestor of present day Delhi.

Based on more recent research done by the Archaeological Society of India, fresh set of excavations have commenced since 2014 in the area of the *Purana Qila* in the quest of the lost Indraprastha of the Mahabharata. But if Vishwakarma's blessings are to be believed, *"this great city will live on forever"*... it still does today in the form of Delhi!

Jalandhar

Jalandhar is a popular city of North India and is one of the important cities of Punjab today, but the city prides in tracing its origins to the mythological and ancient times and we find the history of the place quite well recorded throughout. Jalandhar has passed through the hands of many rulers and dynasties but unlike many cities of the same fate, its name has remained unchanged since the mythical era.

The legend of Jalandhara

The *Shiva Purana* describes Lord Shiva's fight with a mighty *Asura* named Jalandhara, who had defeated the *Devas* and had become the ruler of all the three worlds. Jalandhara had been born out of the ocean and had been thus named. Shiva's battle with Jalandhara was fought in the plains of the North-west and Shiva killed Jalandhara in the battle by crushing his head with a mountain. The region between the Sutlej and Beas rivers is the place where Jalandhara was buried after his death and hence the place is named Jalandhar after him.

Some later ancient texts attribute the origins of Jalandhar to Lav, son of Lord Rama, who is known to have set up his first kingdom in the region. Lav had founded a few cities in the region including Jalandhar, which had been named as it lay between the waters of the two rivers. Jalandhar in *Sanskrit* means 'inside the water'.

Jalandhar in the later Vedic period

Sanskrit grammarian Panini's *Ashtadhyayi* (in V3.116) mentions the *janapada* (district) *Trigarta* as a confederacy of states in the region which corresponds to the later Jalandhar area. The name Trigarta in *Sanskrit* refers to the land drained by three rivers, Ravi, Beas and Sutlej. Trigarta contained *Patanaprastha* (modern day Pathankot) at the entrance of the Kangra valley, and its central portion was made up of the Beas valley and the cities of *Uluka* (ref. Mahabharata – Sabhaparva) (modern day Kulu), *Nagara* (Nagarkot) and *Mandamati* (modern day Mandi). It is said that Nagarkot and the adjacent region was originally founded by Bhima, the second Pandava, and he lived there with his wife Hidimba (this is referenced in the popular folk-lore surrounding the Hidimba temple near Kulu, where Hidimba and her son Ghatotkatch are revered.)

Jalandhar is referred to as the capital for the *janapada* of Trigarta as early as the *Mahabharata* war, in the *Padma Purana*. It remained so, until the region disintegrated during the reign of the *Kushana* king Kanishka in about 100 AD. During the reign of Kanishka, an important Buddhist council was held in Jalandhar which met to collate and arrange the sacred writings of the Buddha and resolve differences within the different sects of Buddhism. During the reign of Emperor Harshavardhana in the 7th Century AD, the Jalandhar doab region was a tributary kingdom to Harsha's empire, ruled over by Raja Udit. The capital remained Jalandhar and a stronghold fort was erected at Kangra. During this time, the Chinese monk and pilgrim Hieuen Tsang visited Jalandhar and his travel accounts mark the presence of considerable Buddhist *stupas* and *viharas* (monasteries) in the region.

In the period after Harsha, when the political chaos in northern and central India kept the kings of different kingdoms engaged in fighting against each other for territorial successes, the north-west region passed into the hands of the *Hindu Shahi* dynasty of Kabul. Jalandhar too was included in their kingdom and was an important city in the *Hindu Shahi* kingdom, the capital of which was Kabul. The *Hindu Shahi* dynasty kings ruled over the entire north-west (part of modern-day Afghanistan, Pakistan and Punjab) for 300 years, while the Kashmir and Himachal areas passed into the hands of the King of Kashmir. Towards the later part of the 10th Century, the *Hindu Shahi* dynasty was overthrown by Mahmud of Ghazni, who invaded the area in 1001 and defeated the *Hindu Shahi* kings of Kabul, Jayapala and Anandapala. It was during his invasion in 1019 that Mahmud captured the fort at Kangra and swept over the area.

The royal family of Jalandhar and Kangra is one of the oldest in India and they claim their descent from the *Chandravanshi* (Lunar dynasty) line of kings. Their genealogy starts with *King Susarma Chandra* who is said to have moved from *Rajputana* and established his kingdom in the Jalandhar doab region. We get to read about many scions of the *Chandra* family between 800 to 1300: from *Jaya Malla Chandra* who was King of Jalandhar in 804, to *King Indra Chandra* who married his daughter to the King of Kashmir in 1028, to the brothers *Hari Chandra* and *Karmma Chandra* who fell to the Muslim rulers expanding and consolidating their kingdoms in Hindustan. Thus we have historical evidence which suggests that Jalandhar existed as an independent state / kingdom for a long time before the invasions and subsequent consolidation of Muslim rule in the region.

Jalandhar: from the medieval to modern period

Jalandhar was first conquered around 1300 by Alauddin Khilji and remained subjugated under his general-in-charge for the region. After Babur invaded and captured Jalandhar, he put Daulat Khan Lodhi in charge of the city as he proceeded further to conquer the heartland of north India. The *Mughal* domination of Jalandhar was briefly interrupted when it passed onto the *Suri* dynasty as Sher Shah overthrew Humayun, but as Humayun made a formidable return to win back his conquered kingdom, the Mughal rule was once again reinstated in Jalandhar and the adjacent region. It remained subjugated to the Mughals till 1750 when the *Durrani* dynasty sultan from Afghanistan captured the city. Maharaja Ghamand Chandra, a Rajput from the *Katoch clan* was placed by the Durranis as the *Nizam of Jalandhar*. However, his rule was short-lived as soon rebellion broke out in the area and by 1760, Jalandhar was being ruled by 12 confederacies of the Sikhs.

By the early 1800s, as the Mughal dynasty lost its power and brilliance and the British started taking control over different kingdoms of India, Jalandhar was annexed by Maharaja Ranjit Singh in 1811. Maharaja Ranjit Singh was a powerful king and a ferocious warrior and extended his sway from the *Waziristan* province in Afghanistan to the *Punjab* in the east.

However, in 1846 Jalandhar was acquired by the British after the first *Anglo-Sikh war* and the Jalandhar cantonment was established. The city became a stronghold of the British in the North-west region, especially in Punjab. There are many tales of valour recorded in Jalandhar's participation in the 1857 mutiny and the later struggles of Indian independence.

Post-independence, Jalandhar became a part of the Indian state of Punjab and served as its capital till 1953, till Chandigarh acquired the status.

Kanyakubja

The story of Kanyakubja sweeps across mythology and history and has a heritage worth its weight in gold and one to be proud of. We find the origins of the city described in mythological texts and its history is well recorded in different Sanskrit classics of the later Vedic period, various royal parchments and also in the accounts of foreign travellers who have visited the ancient city from time to time and have marvelled at its imperial glory.

The mythological era (during the Treta Yuga and before) - the legend of Kanyakubja

The coordinates of Kanyakubja as mentioned in the epic *Ramayana* of the *Treta Yuga,* is briefly as follows:

Jamboodweep (Asia), *Bharat Khand* (India), *Aryavarta desh* (The land of the Aryans, mainly denoting the northern part of India), *Vindhyachaley uttorey* (to the north of the Vindhyachal mountains). The *Valmiki Ramayan, Bal-khand, Sargas 2 and 31 to 33*, gives us a brief history of Kanyakubja and how the city came to get its name as such, and also validates the existence of Kanyakubja in the *pre-Ramayana* mythical era.

One of Lord Brahma's descendants was a King named Kusha from the *Chandravanshi* (Lunar dynasty) line through

Amavasu. Kusha had four sons of whom, Kushanabha, is credited with building a grand city named *Mahodayapura*, in the Indo-Gangetic plains. King Kushanabha's glorious kingdom was called *Madhyadesh* (the central land), chiefly because it occupied the central portion of the *Aryavarta* of the ancient times, with the Vindhyachal mountain range setting its barrier to the south, beyond which the *Aryans* had not ventured till that time. *[The modern day location of Madhyadesh can be estimated to be ranging from Haryana to Uttar Pradesh and western parts of Bihar.]*

Legend has it that King Kushanabha had hundred daughters by his wife Ghritachi, and all of them were divinely beautiful. *Vayu* the wind god was infatuated by them but was rudely rejected by the princesses. In his anger and humiliation Vayu cursed the hundred daughters of King Kushanabha for their haughtiness, as a result of which the daughters developed hunches on their backs, thus deforming their ever-praised physical beauty. Vayu told the King that the curse could only be lifted and the divine beauty of his daughters restored, if a *Brahmin* of upright character married them.

The news of the curse and the fate of the hundred princesses spread like wildfire in the city and across the kingdom. The city *Mahodayapura* soon became to be called *"the city of the hunchback maidens"* or *'Kanyakubja'!* (In *Sanskrit, Kanya* meant daughter and *kubja* meant hunchback). Thus was acquired the name which stayed on as long as the city stood in its glory across the centuries.

After great efforts of frantic search, the King met Brahmadutt, the son of sage Chooli who had set up his abode in the forests nearby and was meditating there. The King explained his predicament and proposed the marriage of his hundred daughters to Brahmadutt. Soon was the marriage was conducted and the moment Brahmadutt touched his hunch-backed wives one by one, their hunches and physical deformity disappeared and their divine beauty was restored, thus ending the curse of Vayu. However, the name Kanyakubja stuck on and the city was thereafter always referred to by this name.

The great Rishi Vishwamitra was the grandson of King Kushanabha but had abdicated the throne of Kanyakubja to his brother Astaka, as he wished to pursue his spiritual cause and pursuit of divine knowledge. The last reference in the mythological texts about Kanyakubja is the mention of King Lauhi, Astaka's son who ruled after his father in King Kushanabha's line.

The Kanyakubja Brahmins

A very important clan of Brahmins, belonging to the Pancha Gauda group of Brahmins of Aryavarta, are the Kanyakubja Brahmins. They trace their ancestry to Rishi Brahmadutt from his marriages to the hundred daughters (princesses) of King Kushanabha of Kanyakubja. The Kanyakubja Brahmins were famous for upholding the traditional Brahminical Hinduism and the Vedic ways of life and propagated Hinduism and the Vedic religious and cultural scriptures and texts, for generations one after another. Sanskrit was their main language and medium of oral and written communication, preaching and authoring texts. They were held in very high esteem and reverence by the Kings of Kanyakubja and were given positions of power in the court and administration, both in the earlier and the later Vedic periods.

The lineage of the Kanyakubja Brahmins are still found in India today though they have scattered across North India, Bihar and Bengal over time. We shall also trace the history of the Kanyakubja Brahmins alongside our main story of Kanyakubja in this article.

Kanyakubja in the Mahabharata era and Earlier Vedic period

There are no direct references to Kanyakubja in the Mahabharata era, but it is often identified with or to be located very near to King Drupad's capital *Kampilya* in the *Dakshin Panchala Pradesh* (South Panchal kingdom). Panchala kingdom was built on the mythical *Madhyadesh* of the dynasty of King Kushanabha and it is also known that the great sage Kapil had his ashram about 30 kms away from the capital Kanyakubja. Kampilya, the most important city in Panchala was also its capital and the venue for the famous *'swayamvara'* ceremony of Draupadi, where Arjun won her hand in marriage.

In the earlier Vedic period, which followed approximately 1000 years after the Mahabharata war, much of the political action was happening in the Indo-Gangetic plains with the Magadha kingdom assuming all the importance and limelight. Panchal Pradesh in the early Vedic period was having a quiet run with its series of local rulers having consolidated the kingdom. Kanyakubja continued with its journey of Vedic learning through the breed of the Kanyakubja Brahmins, however, their agenda of propagating the Hindu scriptures had significantly diminished in the wake of the surge of Buddhism across the country at that period of time.

It was during the reign of the fiery Mahapadma Nanda of the Nanda dynasty around 345 BC that Kanyakubja along with many other cities of *Aryavarta* was won over and annexed to the expanding Magadha kingdom. This was consolidated firmly during the Mauryan period as the entire country from the north-west to the south-east borders was won over by Chandragupta Maurya and his worthy descendants, and the concept of separate *Mahajanapadas* (kingdoms) of the mythological and earlier Vedic times was dissolved to give way to an unified India and provincial heads or capitals therein.

The resultant wide spread of Buddhism and the *Pali* language and their *Prakrits* used extensively during the Mauryan period, forced Hinduism to take a back seat and classical Sanskrit as the language of Vedic literature to be down forced. Thus centres of Hindu scriptural and Vedic learning, like *Kanyakubja*, *Takshashila* and *Girivraja* were affected by the upsurge of Buddhism and later Jainism.

Even as Buddhism surged, in Kanyakubja the Brahmins continued patronising Vedic and scriptural learning in Sanskrit and following the staunch Brahminical Hindu traditions, albeit in a very contained and captive manner. The Kanyakubja Brahmins continued to be the mainstay of the learning and tradition being upheld, but they turned their faces away from the political, social and religious change that was sweeping across the country over these centuries. In the whole scheme of things, Kanyakubja gradually fell into a shadow area but continued its low-profile existence.

Resurgence of Kanyakubja in the Later Vedic period

India was again unified and saw resurgent glorious times under the Gupta Empire (240 AD to 550 AD) and the rise of Brahminical Hinduism was observed during this time. This period is also known as the age of Classical Sanskrit literature. As we have read from the accounts of the Chinese travellers, notably *Fa Hien* in the Mauryan period and *Hiuen Tsang* in the post-Gupta era, along with Taxila, Nalanda and Kanyakubja, other towns such as Mathura, Sarnath, Ujjain, Vidisha and Sravasti were developing as fantastic centres of learning and architecture.

Mathura and Kanyakubja were key towns for the *Madhyadesh* region. Under the Gupta kings, these cities rose to the pinnacle of glory as centres of administration, culture, diverse religions, architecture and celebration of the Classical Sanskrit knowledge. This golden age of the Classical Sanskrit renaissance produced famous litterateurs like *Kalidasa, Bharavi, Sriharsha* and *Magha* who wrote the five *'Mahakavyas'*. Scholars and writers like *Banabhatta, Bhartrihari* and *Vatsyayana* also composed their famous works *Kadambari, the three Shatakas* and *the Kama Sutra* respectively during this time. Further, the Hindu *Puranas* are stated to be composed and refined during this age.

However, in the post-Gupta era (570 AD – 650 AD), Mathura gave way to Kanyakubja, as the latter became important for political reasons and rose to become the capital of King Harsha's undivided Indian empire. However, before Harsha ascended the throne at Kanyakubja, the kingdom was being ruled over by the Varman kings of the Maukhari dynasty who were in constant battle with the Palas of Gauda (Bengal) and the Rashtrakutas of the Deccan, to keep their suzerainty over Kanyakubja.

Kanyakubja as the capital of King Harsha's empire (606 – 647 AD)

Kanyakubja enjoyed its most glorious time during the reign of King Harsha from 606 to 647 AD and was the capital of his empire which ranged from the North-west frontiers to the outer borders of Gauda (Bengal) in the east. Much about Harsha's reign and life is told in the *Harshacharita* composed by his court poet Banabhatta. It is the first historical biography written in Sanskrit language. In the *Harshacharita,* Banabhatta gives an ornate account of life in Harsha's kingdom, his capital Kanyakubja and the adjoining empire. Kanyakubja is portrayed in the most glorified manner as an imperial city un-paralleled in its time and flaunting a deeply rich cultural exchange of literature, religious discourses and practices, surge of Vedic and Sanskrit language and composition of great poetic works. The city is also described to be an important centre of trade and commerce and a destination for many travellers not only from the nearby locations, but also from foreign countries.

The accounts of the famous Chinese pilgrim, Hieuen Tsang, (*a.k.a* Xuanzang) form an important and precious source of information of Harsha's empire and Kanyakubja as his capital city in those times. Hieuen Tsang, being a highly acclaimed Buddhist monk, spent fourteen years in India, travelling to all the sacred places connected with Buddha's life, of which he spent seven years in Kanyakubja, under King Harsha's patronage and hospitality. His accounts acquaint us with the political, religious, economic and social conditions of Kanyakubja in those days. According to Hieuen Tsang, at the time of his visit, he found Nalanda to be on the decline and Kanyakubja and Prayag *(modern day Allahabad)* to be the emerging and vibrant cities. It was exactly in these two places that King Harsha had conducted his two major Religious Assemblies (in 643 AD) during the period of Hieuen Tsang's stay in his kingdom. Hieuen Tsang, in his accounts, writes in great detail about the unmatched brilliance and opulence of Kanyakubja and the benevolence and magnanimity of King Harsha as its ruler, and refers to him by the name *'King Shiladitya'* throughout his writings.

The Kanyakubja Religious Assembly of 643 AD

King Harsha organised a grand religious conference in his capital city of Kanyakubja, on the western banks of the Ganges. The purpose of the assembly was to highlight the teachings of Buddha. This grand function was attended by twenty tributary kings, including the kings of Kamarupa *(modern-day Assam)* Bhaskara Varman from the extreme east, and the King of Vallabhi *(modern day Vallabhipur – near Bhavnagar, Gujarat)* Dhruvasena from the extreme west. Three thousand *Mahayana* and *Hinayana* Buddhists, three thousand Brahmins and Jains, and one thousand Buddhist scholars from the University of Nalanda attended this assembly, which continued for long 23 days. Harsha himself proposed the name of Hieuen Tsang to preside over the assembly. The subject of discussion in the assembly related to *Mahayana* Buddhism.

From the accounts of Hieuen Tsang it is known that a splendid monastery with a shrine was constructed, on the bank of the Ganges for the purpose of the assembly. There, on the huge tower, one hundred feet high, a golden image of Buddha equal to the height of Harsha himself was kept for the view of the large gathering. A smaller image of Buddha, 3 feet in height was every day carried in a procession, joined by all the 20 kings, and with 300 elephants. In that procession, Harsha himself, dressed as the Hindu god *Sakra (referred to as Indra),* held the canopy on the image. The King of Kamarupa, dressed as the god *Brahma*, waved a white fly-whisk around the image.

As the procession progressed, Harsha scattered golden flowers, pearls and gems on all sides for showing honour to the Buddha, Dharma, and Sangha. At the end of the procession every day, Harsha used to wash the image with his own hands at the altar, and carry it on his shoulders to be placed at the appropriate tower. There, the image was dressed in many silken robes, decorated with gems.

Harsha's devotion to the image of Buddha in the Kanyakubja Assembly clearly proves his deep attachment to *Mahayana* Buddhism. The Hindu gods like *Sakra* and *Brahma* were shown as the attendants of Buddha in a symbolic way, since Buddha was considered to be an incarnation of Vishnu.

Kanyakubja in the Later Vedic period... contd. (650 AD – 850 AD)

As Harsha's empire gradually disintegrated after his death, the *Gurjara-Pratiharas* took control of most of Northern India and established the *Pratihara Dynasty*. Nagabhatta I, Nagabhatta II, Ramabhadra and Mihir Bhoja ruled in succession in the powerful *Pratihara* clan with Kanyakubja continuing to be the capital of their empire. They even proclaimed themselves with the title of *'Maharajadhiraja of Aryavarta'* (Great King of Kings of India), having secured the major portion of Northern India under their control.

The *Pratiharas* were staunch Hindu kings and with the decline of Buddhism in the heartland of India after King Harsha's demise, Brahminical Hinduism took centre stage as the predominant religious faith both for the state and its subjects. Kanyakubja and its clan of the Kanyakubja Brahmins therefore continued to enjoy their status of prominence and importance during the next four centuries under the *Pratihara* and *Bhoja* kings.

However, over time in the post-Harsha period, the city's ancient name of *'Kanyakubja'* gradually metamorphosed into the much-colloquial name **'Kannauj'**. How it exactly happened is not documented anywhere, but it is logical to assume that the shortening and rephrasing of the name would have been more due to localised and conversational influences.

[We still know the city by this name. In the present day, **Kannauj** *is located about 75 kms away from Kanpur.]*

The *Pratiharas* did not have a very peaceful reign as there were regular skirmishes with the neighbouring kings either to defend or extend the territories. Kannauj continued to be at the centre of a tripartite power struggle between the *Pratiharas*, the *Rashtakutas* of the South and the *Palas* of the East.

Kannauj: the capital of Aryavarta (836 – 1019 AD)

Kannauj was already well established as the capital of North India from the time of Harsha and with Magadh, Pataliputra, Mathura and other cities fading in their prominence, Kannauj continued to be regarded as the heart of *Aryavarta* and the jewel in the crown most sought after by the kings at war. All of them sought to keep Kannauj under their clamp, as the city strongly signified power and control over *Aryavarta*. The chequered history of war-torn Kannauj during these periods and tales of the battles and coups forged by the *Pratihara, Rashtrakuta* and *Pala* kings over a hundred years is, on one hand fascinating yet on the other, dark and of betrayals and bloodshed.

It was also during this turbulent period that Kannauj once again rose to a commendable height of glory under the Pratihara King, Mihir Bhoja in 836 AD. Though not immediately comparable to the Kannauj under Harsha, Mihir Bhoja ensured that he rebuilt the city's war affected zones and added further magnificence. Learning and culture surged in Kannauj and once again the traditions of Brahmanical

Hinduism were glorified under the Kanyakubja Brahmins, who now had acquired the cult tag of *'Kannaujia Brahmin'*, one that was set to stay for many more centuries to come. Mihir Bhoja's kingdom ranged from the Sutlej River in the North-west to the foothills of Himalayas in the North and from Bengal in the East to Gujarat in the West, while the Narmada River made up for the border in the South. Kannauj was the illustrious capital of his expansive empire and a very prosperous one at that, as we read from the works of *Sulaiman*, the Arab traveller who visited India during this time. Mihir Bhoja also successfully repulsed several Arab invasions on the North-west borders of his kingdom (present day Sindh in Pakistan) and ensured that he united Aryavarta under Kannuj once again, till 885 AD.

Thus in the fight for the control of *Aryavarta* and pursuit of keeping suzerainty over Kannauj as the capital of *Aryavarta*, the Pratiharas had overall emerged victorious against their rivals the Rashtrakutas and the Palas. However, constant wars and break down of kingdoms over this period actually worked against the interests of Aryavarta, for after Mihir Bhoja there was no king who could unite Aryavarta again and build a formidable force.

The first Muslim conquest of Kannauj (1019 AD)

It was in 1018 AD that the tremors of the pounding hoofs of the troops of horsemen of Mahmud of Ghazni's ferocious army were felt on the soil of Kannauj, heralding the most ominous and dreaded of the battles that the magnificent city had ever witnessed. Stories of Mahmud's fearsome invasions and battles on the plains of the Indus and Sutlej had by then spread all across Aryavarta (northern India), as the burly Sultan had already invaded the country at least ten times and indiscriminately killed and looted in the towns and cities that fell in his way.

After conquering Mathura and Mahaban in 1018, Mahmud turned his attention to Kannauj, as he intruded further down the plains. The ruling Pratihara king of Kannauj at that time was Rajyapala who was terrified at the prospect of facing Mahmud's army with the almost certainty of defeat and bloodshed in the capital. Faced with the daunting task of fighting Mahmud's army, Rajyapala chose not to engage in battle with the Sultan and Kannauj was surrendered without a fight. This however did not stop the greedy Sultan from ransacking the city and he proceeded to destroy many important Hindu temples and Buddhist stupas in Kannauj. The holy shrines were desecrated and the temple wealth was looted indiscriminately.

As the pillage and plundering in Kannauj went on at the hands of Mahmud's army, among the subjects the worst fate probably befell the Kanyakubja *(Kannaujia)* Brahmins. On the pretext of *jihad*, the invaders fanatically crushed the Hindu centres of worship and learning, burning Vedic and Sanskrit texts and scriptures wherever they could find them. They were aware that the Brahmins were the keepers of the religious culture and traditions as well as the temple wealth, and hence the wrath fell on them. The Brahmin houses were invaded, destroyed and looted and the priests and scholars were mercilessly tortured, their books and belongings being burnt in front of their eyes. The king had already surrendered and remained a mute spectator as the once glorious city of Kannauj was brought to its knees and its wealth forcibly taken away.

Mahumd of Ghazni left a burning and destroyed Kannauj, and if that wasn't enough, within a year Kannauj was attacked by the neighbouring Chandelas. The rage of the Chandela King was directed against Rajyapala for having meekly surrendered to Mahmud without a fight and for allowing the destruction, arson and looting of his city, but the Chandel soldiers ensured that they also had their share of looting as they ravaged through the already broken city. Rajyapala was killed by the Chandelas and that marked the end of the Pratihara dynasty, leaving Kannauj in a total state of anarchy and political chaos, by the end of 1019 AD.

Revival of Kannauj under the Gahadavala dynasty (1080 – 1200 AD)

The fall of the Pratiharas and the invasions of Sultan Mahmud of Ghazni destroyed the glory of Kannauj. In the ensuing political vacuum of the state, the Chedis, the Paramaras and the Cholas also attacked, destroyed and looted the city of Kannauj, until Chandradeva, a valiant Gahadavala prince of Rajput lineage, defeated them and established sovereignty over Kannauj and the neighbouring areas. From the historical chronicles of the times, it is quoted as follows, that Chandradeva... *"by the valour of his arm acquired the matchless sovereignty over the glorious Kanyakubja"*.

Chandradeva was the first in the Gahadavala dynasty who ruled over Kannauj and made the city the capital of his empire. In yet another verse, Chandradeva of the Gahadavalas is said to be the *"Maharajadhiraja and the protector of the holy places of Kasi, Kanyakubja, Uttarkosala and Indrasthana..."* (*Kasi* being Benaras and *Kanyakubja* being Kannauj, we may understand that *Uttarkosala* referred to the vicinity of Ayodhya; and *Indrasthana* was perhaps Indraprastha – which we know today as Delhi).

It was after Chandradeva's descendant Govindachandra ascending the throne of Kannauj in 1114 AD, that the Gahadavala Empire saw real success once again. Inscriptions found in Sarnath, refer to Govindachandra's military exploits in detail and shower eloquent praise on the young king:

"Maharajadhiraja Govindachandra, it seems is an incarnation of Hari (Lord Vishnu), who has been commissioned by Hara (Lord Shiva) to protect Baranasi (Benaras) from the wicked Turuska (Turkish) warriors, as the only one who is able to protect the earth."

The success of the King of Kannauj is written in bold as *"in consequence of his valiant prowess and the mlechchas (impious or sinful, referring to the invading Turkish armies) vanquished, that there was never any talk of the Hammira (Amir or Sultan) coming back to the banks of the river of the Gods."*

The inscription plates further state that Govindachandra was a devout Shaivite and held the Brahmins in his kingdom in very high esteem. Thus his patronage of the Kanyakubja Brahmins was expansive and large-hearted. It is therefore evident that the Kanyakubja Brahmins once again had days of glory and importance under Govindachandra and the Gahadavala dynasty. Govindachandra's reign was also marked by the rise of literary efforts in Sanskrit, by the Brahmins in his court. His minister for law-and-war, *Lakshmidhara* and another Brahmin minister *Raghunandana* are credited for authoring the very famous Sanskrit work *"Kalpadruma",* a collection of works on law and societal procedures.

Govindachandra ruled for forty years and re-established the glory and magnificence of Kannauj as the capital of the empire, and was succeeded by his son Vijayachandra in 1154. Vijayachandra too like his father stood like a bulwark against the Muslim invaders but did not have much success with his neighbour kings, for when his reign ended in 1170 AD, the Kannauj Empire only extended across the region of modern-day Uttar Pradesh and Bihar.

Vijayachandra's son and successor Jayachandra finds important mention in the history of Kannauj and in that of India for two major incidents that marked the period of his reign: First, the make-believe romantic legend of Prithviraj Chauhan storming into Jayachandra's celebratory event at Kannauj and carrying off his not-unwilling daughter Samyukta for marriage. Second, Jayachandra's valiant resistance of Muhammad Ghori's invasions and his final defeat which led to the destruction of Kannauj by the invading Muslims. The *Purusapariksa* of poet *Vidyapati* describes Jayachandra:

"Yavanesvara Sahavadin (referring to Sihabuddin Ghori) fled several times after sustaining defeat at the hands of King Jayachandra, the 'nikhila-yavana-ksayakarah' (destroyer of all Yavanas – infidels)."

Referring to Jayachandra, the Muslim historian *Ibn Asir* says in his *Kamil-ut-Tawarikh*: *"the King of Kannauj was the greatest in Hind and possessed the largest territory, extending lengthwise from the borders of China to the province of Malwa, and breadthwise from the sea to within ten days journey from Lahore."*

The second Muslim conquest of Kannauj (1194 AD)

Kannauj was swept away and eventually destroyed during the Muslim conquest of Hindustan by the repeated invasions of Sultan Sihabuddin Muhammad Ghori and his Turkic generals. Muhammad Ghori returned in 1194 and with the aid of his slave-general Qutubuddin Aibak, marched towards Kannauj with a very large army. King Jayachandra met Ghori on the plains of Chandwar *(a place between Kannauj and Etawah)* where a pitched battle took place. The tidings of the battle were gradually favouring Jayachandra's army when a freak arrow hit Jayachandra in the eye and pierced his skull, killing him instantly. Seeing their leader dead, the Hindu army scattered directionless and within no time the battle was won by Muhammad Ghori.

As the victorious Sultan reached the outskirts of Kannauj, in the words of an accompanying historian of that time, *"the Sultan there saw an imperial city which raised its head to the skies, and which in strength and structure might justly boast to have no equal. The city was surrounded by strong walls and deep ditches and was washed by the Ganges on its eastern face."*

Ghori plundered and pillaged Kannauj, killing the Hindu populace and breaking the gorgeous temples and shrines while enslaving the people, before retreating with immense war-spoils. After Ghori's exit, Qutubuddin Aibak continued to consolidate the conquered cities by vanquishing the remnants of the Hindu armies in those places. The Rajput resistance however continued in sporadic efforts in different areas in an attempt to throw off the Turkic yoke. In Kannauj, especially, Jayachandra's nineteen year old son, Harishchandra, succeeded in pushing back Aibak's armies and liberated Kannauj once again in 1197 AD, a respite which was destined to be only too short-lived.

The Final Decimation (1211 – 1215 AD)

Post the assassination of Sihabuddin Ghori at Dhamiak near the banks of the Jhelum River in 1206 and the death of Qutubuddin Aibak in 1210, the entire expanse of North India was in political chaos and rebellion. Though Iltutmish, the son-in-law of Qutubuddin Aibak ascended the throne of Delhi and proclaimed himself the next ruler of Hindustan, it took a lot of effort on his part to squash the rebellions and impose his suzerainty over the kingdoms of Hindustan.

Iltutmish's son, Nasir-ud-din Mahmud, a ferocious warrior by his own right, waged a terrible battle against Kannauj, Benaras and Rohilkhand. The battle of Kannauj saw the complete end of the Gahadavala dynasty with the ruling King Harishchandra and his son being driven out of the city, and the establishment of Nasir-ud-din's Turkic generals as administrators of Kannauj. In the pillage, plunder and massacre that ensued in the days of the war, Kannauj was completely destroyed and razed to the ground. The Hindu populace scattered to neighbouring areas and a mass exodus of the Kanyakubja Brahmins were seen in the aftermath of the battle. As Nasir-ud-din and his troop of Turkic generals decimated the city and its remaining people, Kannauj with its heritage and soul of Hindu imperialist tradition, culture and learning was lost forever.

Kannauj thereafter was governed under Nasir-ud-din Mahmud who was appointed as the Governor of Awadh region. The stronghold yoke of the Turkish generals and administrators of the Delhi Sultanate gradually robbed Kannauj of the remnants of its glorious imperial and cultural past. The magnificent city which over the centuries had held pre-eminence in North India and regarded as the seat for many a proud dynasty, ceased to exist as an independent state and slowly sank into insignificance.

Kannauj: Medieval period to modern times

Under the rule of the various Sultans of the Delhi Sultanate and then the Mughals, Kannauj never rose to any significance and remained just another small town, and with the prolonged influence of its rulers, the character of the city underwent a sea-change. Perhaps the only notable mention of the place would be that of Emperor Akbar, who once passing through the place found the soil and environment of Kannauj to be conducive for growing plants which were used to make fragrances (referred to as *Itr*). He ordered for the fragrant plants to be imported from Persia and had them planted in great numbers in the region of Kannauj. Since then till this date, the *'Itr'* of Kannauj is considered heavenly and the best in India. Some even call Kannauj as the *'fragrance capital'* of the country.

In modern times, the city of Kannauj is the administrative headquarters for the district by the same name in Uttar Pradesh, but it stands proud as one of the very few cities in our country to boast of its antiquity and rich heritage.

The following stanza from *Bhartrihari's* composition *'Vairag yasataka' (volume 36)*, is a fitting adieu and lament for Kanyakubja; the epitaph of its glories:

"Alas brother... the mighty kings, the train of barons and witty court at his side, the damsels with faces like the moon's orb, the haughty troop of princes, the minstrels and the tales... by whose will all this hath passed into mere memories... as homage to Time."

Lahore

Although post the partition of India, the city of Lahore became a part of Pakistan, the city has a strong antiquity and a noteworthy past that connects it strongly to the ancient history of undivided India. Thus while writing about the Ancient Cities of India it will be unfair to ignore Lahore and similar cities, even though they are no longer a part of the new India.

Mythical origins and etymology of Lahore

The origins of today's Lahore lie obscured in mythology and can be traced back to the Ramayana era of the *Treta-yuga*. By the end of his reign, Lord Rama and his family were credited with establishing many cities and towns as they kept visiting various parts of their kingdom. One such city was Lavpur, in the basin of the Jhelum River, credited to Lav, son of Lord Rama, as the founder. Lavpur grew in its settlements with Brahmins comprising the majority of its population. There was a temple erected and devoted to Lav in the city, which stands even today empty inside the Lahore fort as the Lav temple.

In the ancient annals of the Rajput clans, who later settled in the region, Lav was called Loh in the local tongue. The Rajputs built a fort at the place to fortify its security and gradually Lavpur came to be known as Lohkot (Loh refers to Lav, and 'kot' meant fort). Even later settlers, mostly during the classical and early Vedic periods called the place as 'Lohawar', (awar was a corrupted form of the Sanskrit word Awarna meaning fort, thus the place name meaning the Fort of Loh.)

The great traveller Al-Idrisi of Morocco refers to ancient Lahore as Lohawar, while Al Beruni in his description of the Himalayas (written around the 10th century AD) says "they can be seen from Lahawar (Lahore)." The ancient mythological references and the different accounts of travellers and historians of the ancient eras sufficiently establish the identity of Lavpur or Lohkot and later Lohawar as the city of Lahore and its etymology. In whatever form the ancient name of Lahore may have been written and called, it is manifest that the name has a clear reference to its mythical founder Lav, the son of Rama.

Prominence of Lahore in history – 9th Century AD and later

Lahore came into prominence as a city and province in the 9th Century during the Hindu Shahi Empire of Kabul. [Incidentally, the city of Kabul too has a mythical origin and is said to have been founded by Lord Rama himself on the banks of Kapul River, from which it derives its name. Kabul has had a chequered but a very interesting journey in its ancient history, but that's for another day!] The Hindu Shahi dynasty ruled from Kabul over parts of Afghanistan, Pakistan and Kashmir areas, for about 300 years and was the last Hindu empire of the region, before being conquered and over thrown by the invading armies of Mahmud of Ghazni in 1000 AD.

During the reign of the Hindu Shahi dynasty in the region, Lahore was part of their empire and a prominent province on the east of the River Irawa (Ravi). Lahore was their last capital after they were driven out of Waihind by Mahmud's forces in 1001. The Hindu Shahi ruler Anandapala is referred to as 'Hakim-e-Lahur' by some Muslim historians of the time. In the 'Hudud-i-Alam' (Regions of the World) written around the same time, Lahore is described as "a shehr inhabited by non-Muslims and having impressive temples, large markets and huge orchards."

The Muslim conquests of Lahore

Sultan Mahmud of Ghazni conquered Lahore after a long siege and fierce battle in 1021. During the battle, the city is said to have been burnt, suffered extensive damage and was depopulated. Mahmud established Malik Ayaz as the governor of Lahore and Ayaz was able to rebuild the city and bring back the settlements. Over the period of the next 150 years, Lahore became a centre of learning and culture and gained prominence in Persian poetry. Many acclaimed Persian poets and litterateurs of the time migrated to Lahore from different places and settled here. In the words of a contemporary historian, "Lahore was the Ghazni of India… it had as more Persian poets than any other Islamic city".

Sihabuddin Muhammad Ghori took over Lahore after defeating the last line of the Ghaznavid rulers and viceroys and established Nasir-ud-din Qabacha as the governor of Punjab, who also ruled over Lahore. However, after Ghori's death, his slave general Qutbuddin Aibak overthrew Qabacha and ascended the throne of the Delhi Sultanate at Lahore in 1206. Over the next 300 years, Lahore remained part of the Delhi Sultanate and was governed by different rulers from the dynasties of the Khiljis, Tughlaqs, Sayyids, Lodhis and Suris, until the Mughal rule began.

Lahore in the Mughal era

Lahore was a favourite city of the Mughal Emperors who regarded it on the same ranks of Delhi and Agra. The Mughals made Lahore their winter capital, to escape the extreme winters of Delhi and extensively beautified the city with palaces, gardens and mosques.

Emperor Akbar is credited with building many palaces and the notable architectural marvel, the Daulat Khana-e-Aam (the Hall of Audience for the public), which had one hundred and fourteen porticos. Akbar also tried to bring in a synthesis of religions in Lahore by building religious buildings for different religions. Akbar's son and successor Prince Salim (Jahangir) was also very fond of Lahore. He is said to have been greatly enamoured by the beautiful courtesan Anarkali in Lahore. The make-believe and legendary romantic tale of Salim and Anarkali has been the subject of many shayari and ghazals, being truly epitomized in the famous Bollywood movie Mughal-E-Azam. The tombs of both Anarkali and Jahangir are in Lahore, though in different parts of the city.

The architectural brilliance and spree of Lahore reached its peak during the reign of Shahjahan. He like his ancestors built quite a few palaces and gardens in Lahore, including the famed Shalimar Bagh. Shahjahan is also credited with building the Delhi Gate in the Lahore Fort facing the direction of Delhi, and a similar Lahori Gate in the Red Fort in Delhi, facing the direction of Lahore. The concept was to lay a direct road between the two cities starting with these Gates on either end. Shahjahan's son, Aurangzeb constructed Lahore's most famous mosque, the Badshahi Masjid and the Alamgiri Gate.

Lahore after the Mughals

The period after the decline of the Mughals once again saw Lahore plunged into political chaos. Nader Shah of Persia invaded India in 1739 and pillaged all the towns that fell on his way, Lahore had no escape from his wrath and loot. Soon after, the Durranis from Afghanistan invaded and Ahmed Shah Abdali captured Lahore and annexed the city. The Marathas saw this as an opportunity and extended their intention of capturing Delhi and the north of India onto Lahore. They successfully drove out the Durrani's but the Maratha rule over Lahore was quite short-lived, as the Durrani's returned with a vengeance. Amidst the political chaos and the battles for supremacy, the confederacy of the Sikh misls led by Maharaja Ranjit Singh made gains as they defeated the Durranis in a battle between Lahore and Amritsar and successfully drove the Durranis out. Maharaja Ranjit Singh built his empire across the Punjab region and ruled from Lahore, till the Anglo-Sikh wars that saw the passing of Punjab into the hands of the British.

Lahore in the British Raj era

Legend has it that Maharaja Ranjit Singh had obtained the famous Kohinoor Diamond from the defeated Durrani ruler and brought it with him as he set up the capital of the Sikh empire in Lahore. In a sense, for the next few generations, as Maharaja Ranjit Singh and his descendants ruled over Lahore, the city was home to the world's most precious diamond. The Kohinoor diamond had been officially willed by Maharaja Ranjit Singh to be sent to the Lord Jagannath Temple in Puri (Odisha), but the British did not allow his will to be executed after his death. At the end of the second Anglo-Sikh war when Punjab was annexed to the British Raj, the Kohinoor was taken from the family treasury by the British officers and ceded to Queen Victoria through the 'Last Treaty of Lahore' in 1839. The youngest son of Maharaja Ranjit Singh, the nine-year-old new and titular Maharaja, Duleep Singh, had absolutely no authority or control but to part with the diamond to the British governor general Lord Dalhousie.

The British established new garrisons and installed army cantonments in Lahore, as for them the city was a frontier town sharing borders with Afghanistan and Persia. The region was re-designated as the 'North-west Frontier Province' with Lahore as its capital. Under the British, Lahore saw re-development and surge of colonial architecture, which was a mix of Mughal, Gothic and Victorian styles. Sir Ganga Ram, who is often referred to as the 'father of modern Lahore', designed and built new buildings and clock towers in the city.

Lahore: during the Independence struggle

Lahore deserves a special mention in the Independence movement of India. It was in the 1929 Indian National Congress session held in Lahore that the motion of Declaration of Indian Independence was first tabled and unanimously passed. At the midnight of 31st December 1929, for the first time the current tricolour (the present National Flag of India) was hoisted in Lahore as a National Flag and was saluted by a huge congregation of people. Subhash Chandra Bose is known to have stayed in Lahore during his escape from the clutches of the British, on his way to Europe to garner support for the Indian independence movement.

The British prison in Lahore was a much feared one for its dungeons and excruciatingly harsh treatment meted out to the Indian freedom fighters. Noted freedom fighter Jatin Das died in the Lahore prison after fasting for 63 days in protest of the harsh treatment by the British to the political prisoners. One of the greatest martyrs in the Indian Independence struggle, Shaheed Sardar Bhagat Singh was hanged inside Lahore prison.

In 1940, in another session, Muhammad Ali Jinnah of the then All India Muslim League first presented the 'Two-Nation theory' to the British and demanded the creation of Pakistan. Lahore was the capital of 'undivided Punjab' till then, and hence after the partition and independence, when Lahore became part of Pakistan, the Indian state of Punjab chose Jalandhar as its capital (later moved to Chandigarh in 1953).

Multan

The present city of Multan in the heartland of modern-day Pakistan finds its origins firmly in ancient Indian mythology and traces its history through a wonderful heritage worthy of note.

The mythological origins and etymology of Multan

Multan derives its name from its *Sanskrit* name ***Mulasthana***, but before we come to that, let us first explore the myths related to the city's origins.

The city is said to be founded by the great Rishi Kashyap – one of the *Saptarishis*. Kashyap was married to Daksha's daughters Aditi and Diti. Through his first wife Aditi, he begot the *Agni* (Fire) and Aditya (Sun) clan of sons, while through his second wife Diti, he begot the *Daitya* (*Asura* / Demon) clan of sons. The city which Kashyap founded as their home was named **Kashyapapura**, situated in the plains between the lower Chenab and Sutlej rivers. However, Kashyap was succeeded by his *Daitya* son Hiran Kashyap, who was succeeded by his son Prahlad, who then was succeeded his son Banasura. It is said that later Krishna had killed Banasura and placed his son Shamba on the throne of Kashyapapura.

The legend of Prahlad

The story of the haughty and unjust king Hiran Kashyap

and his son Prahlad is a very popular folklore in India from a very long time. Being an *Asura* king, Hiran Kashyap could not bear the fact that his son Prahlad would worship Lord Vishnu. However, Prahlad was a dedicated devotee of Vishnu and was protected by the Lord from the wrath of his father. The legend has it that Lord Vishnu adopted the avatar of *Narasimha* (man-lion) and broke through a pillar of the palace and killed Hiran Kashyap tearing his body with his claws. Even the legend of the treachery of Prahlad's aunt Holika intending to throw Prahlad into the fire, is also quite popular.

It is believed that Hiran Kashyap's palace where Vishnu appeared in the *Narasimha* avatar, was at Kashyapapura. The **Prahladpuri temple** in the city was built by Prahlad himself and the deity of *Narasimha* was worshipped there. It was a very popular temple throughout the ages and a pilgrimage site for the Hindus, who also believed that the ritual of '*Holika Dahan*' and the celebrations in the form of *Holi* were also started in Kashyapapura in the mythological age.

The Hindu heritage of Multan

During the later mythological period, or the *Mahabharata* era, the region was ruled over by King Malla of the *Chandravanshi* (Lunar dynasty) line of kings. His tribe was known as the Malli's who resided in the area of Kashyapapura. Thus the place was named as *Mallisthana* (the place of the Malli's) which was later adapted in conversational Sanskrit to *Mulasthana*, from which the present name **Multan** is derived.

It is however interesting to note that people of the Malli tribe were originally Rajput Katoch people who adopted Kashyap as their *Gotra* (lineage) from Rishi Kashyap, thus keeping the name of the city's founder alive.

Multan, from the ancient times itself was a place known for its impressive Hindu temples. The *Aditya Sun Temple* in Multan was considered to be one of the largest Hindu temples of its time, and could house 6000 people at a single time. It was dedicated to *Aditya*, the Sun-god of Hindu mythology, but apart from the Hindu pilgrims it also attracted people of Persia who in the Zoroastrian faith worshipped *Mithra* – cult of the Sun.

The Sun Temple of Multan is believed to have been built by Sambha, Sri Krishna's son as a homage to *Surya*, the Sun god, for curing him of leprosy which was inflicted on him as a curse by Sage Durvasa. Thus, it was widely believed that the golden idol of *Aditya* in the Sun Temple of Multan could cure maladies.

Hieuen Tsang, the Chinese traveller and Buddhist monk visited Multan in 641 AD and after visiting the Sun Temple wrote that *"the Aditya Surya Temple is by far the largest temple in India. The idol of Aditya was made of pure gold with his eyes made of large red rubies. Gold, silver and gems have been abundantly placed in the temple's doors, walls, pillars and shikhara (tower). Thousands of Hindus regularly come to Multan to worship the Sun god."* Hieuen Tsang also mentions having seen groups of *Devadasi's* (dancing girls) in the temple at the time of worship and other functions. Other travellers who visited the temple mention that idols of Shiva and Buddha were also installed in the temple. Overall, the ancient sources all provide a glowing description of the Sun temple of Multan.

In the 8th Century, when Multan saw its first conquest at the hands of the *Umayyad Caliphate* under the leadership of Muhammad bin Qasim, the Sun Temple was "carefully protected" by the city's rulers. The earning from the temple offerings used to account for about 30% of the kingdom's revenue, and the fact that the temple was such a highly regarded and famous place of pilgrimage of the Hindus made the rulers take precious care of it.

However, during the mid-900's Multan was conquered and occupied by the *Qarmatian Ismaili Shias*, who were infamous for having notoriously destroyed, plundered and killed pilgrims at the holy *Kabba* shrine in Mecca. Under their fearsome leader Jalam bin Shayban, the new *Ismaili Shia* ruler of Multan, the gorgeous Sun Temple of Multan was completely destroyed, the golden idol of Aditya was hammered to pieces and all the temple wealth pillaged. The *Ismaili Shias* built a congregational mosque atop the decimated Sun temple, which in turn was looted and destroyed by Sultan Mahmud of Ghazni (due to his hatred against the *Shia* Muslims) when he attacked Multan in the 11th Century. During Mahmud's attack, his accompanying historian Al Beruni, wrote in glowing words about the Sun Temple, though by then the temple was already destroyed.

The *Prahladpuri* temple in Multan, (mentioned earlier in this article) had also been destroyed multiple times during the Muslim conquests of Multan, and by the 19th Century had become a nondescript shrine, being barely managed by group of influential Hindus in the city. A mosque had also been built within the original temple premises. During the Sikh era of 1810, the temple had been restored to some extent, but again in the Colonial era, it was damaged during gun-shelling on Multan by the British armies. Finally, during partition and creation of Pakistan in 1947, the then *Mahant* of the temple, Baba Narayan Das Batra, carried the *Narsimha* and *Prahlad* idols of the temple from Multan and placed them in a new temple in Hardwar.

The *Prahladpuri* temple thereafter lay vacant with some local Hindu groups making efforts to upkeep the temple structure. But during the 1992 *Ayodhya Babri-Masjid* demolition episode, retaliatory attacks were made on the remains of the *Prahladpuri* temple structure by Islamic extremist groups in Multan after which the temple fell to ruins completely.

Muslim rule era in Multan

The Muslim conquest and consolidation of Multan started with the *Umayyad Caliphate* as early as the 8th Century, followed by the ruthless rulers of the *Qarmatian Ismaili Shias* and then Mahmud of Ghazni who annexed the city to his Ghaznavid Empire in 1005. Muhammad Ghori took Multan in 1175, when he expelled the *Ismaili Shias* who had asserted their independence from Ghazni in the meantime. Later Multan passed on to be governed by the Delhi Sultanate, established by Qutbuddin Aibak and consolidated by Iltutmish. The later dynasties of the Khiljis,

Tughlaqs, Saiyyads, Lodhis and Suris all had Multan under their control.

It was under the **Mughal Empire** in 1525 that Multan saw development and enjoyed a reign of peace for almost 200 years. The city grew under the Mughal patronage such that it came to be known as *Dar Al-Aman* (the Abode of Peace). The *Khakwani Nawabs of Multan* who were the governors of the city under the Mughals gave it strong financial stability, boost for the economy and promoted agriculture and industry in the area. In line with the Mughals' love for architecture, many beautiful and important buildings and palaces were built in Multan during this time. The influence of the Sufi saints during this time in the region saw the peaceful spread of Islam and of Muslim religious and cultural impact over Multan.

Post the decline of the Mughals, the North-west region saw the invasion of the Afghan kings of the **Durrani** dynasty. Ahmed Shah Abdali led the charge which was carried forward by his son and successor Timur Shah Durrani, who was defeated and thrown out by the **Maratha** general Raghunathrao. Multan thereafter passed under the control of the Marathas for a short while. While the rest of Punjab soon saw the rise of the Sikh Confederacy *misls* and their supremacy, the Saddozai, Khokhar and Khatri Muslim rulers of Multan and defended the city successfully against the repeated attacks by the Sikh *misls*.

It was only in the early 19th Century that Maharaja Ranjit Singh with his capital in Lahore, attacked and occupied Multan. His general, Hari Singh Nalwa defeated and killed the ruler of Multan, Muzaffar Khan Saddozai and established the **Sikh** empire control on Multan, with which the Muslim rule of Multan came to an end.

Multan in the Colonial Era and modern times

The famous *Siege of Multan* by the **British** began in April 1848, when rebellion sparked under the leadership of Diwan Mulraj Chopra. After a long and bloody battle which lasted for almost a year, the British finally managed to breach the Multan fort and capture the city and Multan became part of the British Raj in January 1849.

The British made some concerted efforts to enhance industrialization in Multan and set up railway connectivity, but the development did not meet with much success.

During the Independence movement and creation of Pakistan, Multan's predominantly Muslim population supported the All India Muslim League. The partition of 1947 saw many Hindus and Sikhs migrating from Multan to India and many Muslims came over to settle in Multan. The city today continues as one of the most important urban centres in southern Punjab of Pakistan.

Nandana

The city of *Nandana* and the Nandana Fort was founded by Anandapala, a powerful king in the line of the **Hindu Shahi** dynasty of Kabul, estimated around 1005 AD. Nandana is located on the verdant valley on the eastern flanks of the Salt Range hills in the Punjab region of (modern-day) Pakistan. The city had a very short life, but is an important one in the context of the Kabul Hindu Shahi dynasty lineage, being its last capital before its decimation in war.

The Hindu Shahis of Kabul

The *Shahis* of Kabul ruled over the Kabul valley and extended surrounding regions from the 4th to the 11th Century, and were classified in history into two broad eras, viz., the Kabul Shahis and the Hindu Shahis.

The Kabul Shahi dynasty commenced right after the Kushana rule in that region *(famous for King Kanishka)* in the 4th Century. At that time, Kabul and the upper North-west region (modern-day north Afghanistan) was inhabited by people of mixed races who practised different faiths. The line of the Hindu Kambojas *(initiated into Hinduism at the time of the Ramayana – said to be by Lord Rama himself when he founded the city of Kabul)* were prominent, while Bamiyan and Kabul also had strong influences of Buddhism, albeit on the decline. While Hinduism and Buddhism were the primary faiths practised in the region, the culture of the people was quite influenced by the Turkic interactions of its western neighbours.

The Kabul Shahi rulers were often harassed by wars against them by Turkic Muslim armies across their western borders. In 671, during one such invasion when the Muslim armies invaded Kabul, the capital was shifted to *Uddabhandapura,* situated further east towards the Kashmir valleys.The Kabul Shahi kings were Hindu-Kshatriyas, and had illustrious Hindu ministers and generals in their court and army. During the attack and destruction of *Takshashila*, (India's first global university and seat of learning), the Kabul Shahi kings had given shelter to many Buddhist monks and Hindu Brahmins who had fled there. It was one such Brahmin minister Kallar *(a.k.a Lalliya)* in the court of the last Kabul Shahi king Lagaturman, who effected a *coup d'etat* and overthrowing the king, installed himself as the ruler. The lineage of Kallar, who were Brahmins who gave up their priestly duties and took up martial arts, were known as the Hindu Shahi dynasty of Kabul.

The Hindu Shahi dynasty began their reign in 870 AD. King Jayapaladeva was one of their most significant kings and was the contemporary of the Turk ruler Sebuk Tigin of Ghazni and his son Mahmud (977 – 1001). His kingdom stretched from Laghman to Kashmir and from Sirhind to Multan, coving an expansive tract of land. However, he continued to have repeated battles with Mahmud of Ghazni on territorial supremacy in the region, as the Ghaznavid Empire and the Hindu Shahi kingdom shared borders. King Jayapala was once and for all decisively defeated by Mahmud in 1001 and he self-immolated himself on the funeral pyre to escape capture and forced conversion to Islam at the hands of Mahmud. Kabul was invaded, destroyed and annexed to the Ghaznavid Empire and thus forever lost to the Hindu Shahis.

King Anandapala, son and successor of Jayapala ascended the throne in 1002 and continued to reign the Hindu Shahi kingdom, but within a few years, his capital Uddabhandapura was also attacked, invaded and annexed by Mahmud, forcing him to retreat further south towards Lahore.

Foundation of Nandana

It was during the time of King Anandapala's reign in Lahore that the idea of setting up a fortress city on the hills came to his mind. Some historians say that Anandapala wanted to take advantage of the Salt Range hills strategically and was at the same time lulled by the pristine beauty of the verdant valleys in that area.

Thus, around 1005, he built the city of **Nandana** on the hills of the Salt Range, with a fort placed strategically to protect and provide resistance to the invading armies. The city, though not a large one, had decent population and gradually grew popular more for its wonderful location and views than for anything else, until one day it became the capital of the Hindu Shahi kings. Its founder King Anandapala is credited to have built a Shiva temple on the highest part of the hill city, the ruins of which still stand today. The King named this city *'Nandana'* after the divine mythical garden present in *Lord Indra's* palace in heaven, thus symbolically praising the natural beauty and divinity of the city.

Anandapala's foresight had proved him right, as Mahmud returned to attack and continued to inflict heavy losses on the Hindu Shahi kingdom. The *Battle of Chach* was Anandapala's last stand against Mahmud of Ghazni, post which he signed a tributary treaty with the victorious Sultan. After Anandapala's death in 1010, his son Trilochanapala succeeded him.

The end of Nandana

King Trilochanapala ascended the throne in 1011 but of a much-reduced kingdom. In his endeavour to expand the territories of his kingdom, he waged wars with other Hindu kings of north India and was successful in extending his kingdom to the upper Yamuna plains and into the Sivalik hills. However, during Mahmud of Ghazni's later campaigns in India when he attacked Mathura and Kannauj, some of Trilochanpala's own mutinous troops who fought in his army against Mahmud, assassinated him.

Bheempala succeeded his father Trilochanapala to the throne of the Hindu Shahis in 1021, but by this time the Hindu Shahi kingdom was reduced only to their capital city of Nandana. The empire was at its lowest, but Bheempala ruled over the city of Nandana peacefully for five years. In 1026, in the fierce *Battle of Nandana*, Bheempala personally commanded his troops in defence of his city, fought valiantly and seriously wounded the commander of the Ghaznavid army, Muhammad bin Ibrahim. The record of the battle of Nandana is described by the contemporary Muslim chronicler *Utbi* in his work where he describes King Bheempala as *"King Bheem, the fearless... fought with courage and valour..."*

The city of Nandana was taken, ravaged and looted by the Ghaznavid army and King Bheem was killed in the battle. The city being completely destroyed, was gradually depopulated and fell to ruins eventually being erased from its once beautiful location atop the Salt Range hills.

The *Battle of Nandana* not only saw the end of the last capital of the Hindu Shahi dynasty being wiped out, but the entire dynasty itself collapsed and ended. King Bheempala therefore was the last king of the once famed Hindu Shahi dynasty. Bheempala's descendants served as generals and courtiers in Kashmir. They gained positions of prominence in the royal court of Kashmir and intermarried with the royal family. In the subsequent battles which the King of Kashmir fought against Mahmud of Ghazni, one of Bheempala's sons, Rudrapala, finds mention in the description of the war by Kalhana, a 12th century Kashmiri Brahmin and author of *Rajatarangini,* as being *"a valiant general in the battlefield..."*

Nandana: modern times

Whilst since 1026, the city of Nandana fell to ruins after its destruction, there have hardly been any mention or reference to it. However, in the last few decades with proper excavations being conducted in the Salt Range hills, the city is being rediscovered. Today only the ruins of the *Nandana*

Fort and the *Shiva temple* built by King Ananadapala, the founder of Nandana, stand as testimony to this once beautiful and short-lived ancient city and its claim to heritage and history.

Oudh

Oudh was once a princely state located in the Awadh region of northern India. Whilst the place has its origins deeply entrenched in mythology, it also acquired fame and prominence during the medieval and Mughal periods of Indian history. During the time of the British Raj, the state was popular by its name Oudh, but this name gradually became obsolete with disuse. That the princely state of Oudh thereafter merged with the larger region of Awadh was also one of the reasons of the name not being used any more.

Etymology of Oudh

The name Oudh is derived from its most prominent city and capital Ayodhya. In Sanskrit, the name Ayodhya means *'one that cannot be fought against'* or simply *'invincible'*. The state was formed around Ayodhya and thus got its name Oudh as an adjective, *'.... of Ayodhya'*. This naming is validated in the *Atharvaveda* which refers to Ayodhya as the *'invincible city of the gods'*.

Oudh, however, was a lesser known name and the place was more popularly known as *'Awadh'*, which is also derived from Ayodhya. From the etymology and name variants over the eras, one can understand the immense importance attached to this city at all times, that the immediate state and province of which Ayodhya was the capital, derived their names from it.

Origin of Oudh (or Ayodhya) in mythology

As stated in the *Puranas*, the city was created by Manu (progenitor of all mankind in this time-cycle) and handed over to Ikshvaku to rule. Ikshvaku was the first of the *Suryavanshi* (Solar dynasty) line of Kings and the first King of *Aryavarta* (northern India). Further details and description of Ayodhya is provided elaborately in the epic *Ramayana* which bases its story in the city. The region is described in the *Ramayana* (7th century BC) as the expansive kingdom of Kosala, with Ayodhya as its capital where King Dashrath ruled in the *Suryavanshi* line of kings as Ikshvaku's descendants. Ayodhya is famous as Lord Rama (son and successor of King Dashrath) was born there and ruled the kingdom for many years post his return from exile, where he established golden societal laws in an endeavour to create the utopian society, *'Ram-rajya'*.

At the end of his reign Lord Rama is said to have divided his kingdom into two, North and South Kosala, with capitals at *Sravasti* and *Kusavati* and entrusted them to his two sons to rule. Lord Rama himself entered into the waters of the Sarayu River along with all the inhabitants of the city and ascended to heaven. It is said that after Lord Rama's ascent to heaven, Ayodhya became desolate and insignificant. A local belief attributes the cause to the mass suicide which made Ayodhya empty.

Ayodhya was revived again by King Vikaramaditya who ruled in 50 BC from Sravasti. Vikramaditya originally hailed from Ujjain and Ayodhya became a populated city once again during his time, though the capital of the kingdom remained at Sravasti. Ayodhya retained its fame as the birthplace of Lord Rama and thus became an important pilgrimage centre for the Hindus. The *Brahmanda Purana* includes Ayodhya in the list of the seven holiest cities for the Hindus, along with Mathura, Hardwar, Kashi, Kanchi, Dwarka and Avantika. The Buddhists and Jains also hold Ayodhya in great reverence as the Buddha is said to have meditated and preached in Ayodhya, while five Jain Tirthankaras were born in the city.

Ayodhya again saw a rise during the medieval period when the *Gahadavalas* ruled the region. Though the capital at that time was Kannauj, the empire included the Oudh region. The *Gahadavalas* were *Vaishnavites* and thus upheld the cult of Rama as the incarnation of Vishnu. With the widespread rise and popularity of Vaishnavism, Ayodhya was emphasized as an important centre and the seat of Lord Rama.

Oudh during the Mughal period

By the time the Mughals came to rule, the region was called the province of Awadh, and the city of Ayodhya was thriving and an important pilgrim centre. The city by then had also seen a spate of damage and destruction in the wars between the initial Mughals and the local rulers. The (much disputed) *Babri Masjid* was built at Ayodhya, at the behest of the first Mughal emperor Babur when he invaded the city. It was during the time of the later Mughals that Awadh rose in importance as a province and Ayodhya remained its capital.

Towards the end of the Mughal period, in 1732, Saadat Ali Khan, the subah-governor of Awadh under the Mughals gave himself the title of *Padshah* (King) and proclaimed independence. He started the famous lineage of the Nawabs of Awadh and they continued their sway and administration over the region till Awadh was annexed by the British in 1856.

Saadat Ali Khan laid the foundation of a new city Faizabad, which was on the outskirts of Ayodhya. Faizabad became the capital during the reign of the third Nawab of Awadh, Shuja-ud-Daula. The Awadh province being the granary of north India was extremely prosperous and the Nawabs lived a grand and extravagant lifestyle. Awadh was one of the richest provinces of India at that time and was ruled independently. Shuja-ud-Daula was defeated by the British at the *Battle of Buxar* and had to pay huge compensations to the East India Company, including cessation of parts of his territory.

The fourth Nawab, Asaf-ud-Daula, moved the capital of Awadh from Faizabad to Lucknow in 1775, which laid the foundations of a great city. Lucknow since continued as the capital of Awadh, even in the British period, as well as post-Independence. On a related note, Lucknow traces its origins to the mythological *'Lakshmanavati'* as a city founded by Rama's brother Lakshman in the *Ramayana* times. Later, the town was popularly known as *'Lakhnauti'* from where the present name Lucknow is derived.

It is during this time that the British started taking serious interest in Awadh. The province is referred to as Oudh, by the British in all their documents and correspondence. The British finally annexed Oudh to their Raj in 1856 through the *Doctrine of Lapse*, deposing the then Nawab, Wajid Ali Shah. The Nawab was exiled to Calcutta where he built a marvellous palace in the Metiabruz area on the outskirts of the main city. The palace is said to be a miniature model of the Nawab's palace in Lucknow.

Culture and cuisine of Oudh

Oudh, or Awadh as it was called during the times of the Nawab, was famous for its cultural extravaganza. Poets, singers, musicians and courtesans thronged the court of the Nawabs while *'shayari'* and *'ghazal'* flowed in Urdu and Persian through the veins of Awadh. The province soon acquired the famous epithets *'Shaam-e-Awadh'* (evenings of Awadh) for its beautiful sunsets and evenings and *'Tehzeeb ki Nagri'* (city of courteousness) for the extra-polite behaviour and exchanges that people exhibited in general. The famous Bollywood movie *'Umrao Jaan'* is made on the life-story of an extremely popular courtesan of Awadh in the times of the *Nawabi,* the story of her admirers across Awadh, Faizabad and Lucknow being legendary.

Cuisine was yet another aspect that Awadh was richly famous for. With strong influence of the Mughal kitchens, *Awadhi* cuisine soon made a signature mark of its own. The *bawarchis* and *rakabdars* of Awadh brought about the *'dum'* style of cooking over a low fire and their regular spread would include delicacies like kebabs, kormas, biriyani, kaalia, nahari-kulcha, zarda, sheermal, taftan, roomali rotis and warqi paranthas. The food was rich not only in its ingredients but also the flavoured spices used in its preparations. Legend has it that Nawab Wajid Ali Shah was accompanied by his cooks in his exile to Calcutta and when the Nawab could no longer afford sufficient mutton for his biriyani, the cooks substituted it with the potatoes they found in Bengal. This new innovation of the *Awadhi Biriyani* with potatoes still lives on, popular today as the *Kolkata Biriyani!*

Oudh in the times of Independence

The British soon had annexed the neighbouring provinces, and when post the 1857 rebellion, Delhi fell to them, they exiled the last Mughal Emperor Bahadur Shah Zafar to Rangoon. Oudh at that time no longer remained a separate province, but was merged with the *United Provinces of Agra* and was ruled over by the British Resident Officer.

After independence, the names Oudh and Awadh have remained only in historical records, local culture and conversational references. Lucknow is now referred to as the seat of the erstwhile Oudh or Awadh, having been the capital of the Nawabs of Awadh, but the true Oudh still remains inclusive of both the *Nawabi Lucknow* and the *mythological Ayodhya.*

Peshawar

Peshawar, the capital of the *Khyber Pakhtunkhwa* province in Pakistan, boasts of a rich history which dates back to 539 BC. Peshawar has seen many rulers and dynasties and has also been patronised by many. Peshawar's history is well recorded and thanks to the excavations conducted in the area during the British Raj and other times, we also have notable evidence in support.

The founding and etymology of Peshawar

Peshawar was founded as the ancient city of *Purushapura,* which in Sanskrit means *'the city of men'*. It was founded on the *Gandhara* plains as a small village settlement in about 539 BC. Its location was near to *Pushkalavati,* the capital of the *Gandhara* kingdom. Along with *Pushkalavati, Takshashila* (Taxila) and *Varmayana* (Bamyan), *Purushapura* completed the list of important cities in ancient *Gandhara.*

The noted Arab historian *Al-Masudi* noted that by the 10th century AD, the name of the city had come to be known as *Parashawar*, a name which continued for a few more centuries, till the Mughal Emperor Akbar changed its name to Peshawar.

The Buddhist heritage of Peshawar

In 326 BC when Alexander the Great subdued the kings

of the region and conquered the Peshawar valley, the area came under the control of Seleucus I Nicator and was a part of his Seleucid Empire. However, following the battle and subsequent treaty between Chandragupta Maurya and Seleucus, along with a large part of the North-western territories, Peshawar was also ceded to Chandragupta and was included in the Mauryan Empire. It was during the time of Ashoka the Great that the entire *Gandhara* region was entrenched in Buddhism. From many Buddhist monasteries dotted across *Gandhara* and its cities *(modern day central Afghanistan and north Pakistan),* and innumerable stupas, to the rock-cut mammoth statues of the Buddha at Bamyan, the region was sweeping in Buddhist culture.

Another proponent of Buddhism was the *Kushana* king Kanishka, who ruled over the region and made Peshawar his capital in 128 AD. A devout Buddhist, Kanishka built the grand *Kanishka Mahavihara*, an expansive monastery in the region, the ruins of which are still seen today. After his death, a massive *Kanishka Stupa* was built in Peshawar to house Buddhist relics. By 232 AD, the Kushana rule ended in Peshawar and soon after the city was attacked by the armies of the *Sassanids* under Shapur I. They caused extensive damage to the Buddhist monastery and also destroyed the monumental stupa. Later during the time of the 400s, when the *White Huns* took over Peshawar and were ruling from there, the *Kanishka Stupa* was restored to some extent.

In the words of Chinese traveller *Fa Hien* who visited Peshawar during this period, the *Kanishka stupa* was *"the highest of all the towers in the terrestrial world."* During the Kushana period, the population of Peshawar was estimated to be 120,000 thus making it the world's seventh most populated city at that time. However, when Hieuen Tsang visited Peshawar around 630 AD, the city had seen few centuries of conflict among the Huns and other Pashtun tribes thus reducing its population and also its grandeur. Hieuen Tsang wrote in lament on seeing the ruins of the Buddhist monasteries and stupas, *"the city and its great Buddhist monuments have decayed to ruin."*

Islamic rule in Peshawar

Peshawar in the 7th century passed on to the hands of the *Kabul Hindu Shahi* rulers for some time, but as their powers dwindled, different Pashtun tribes took over the city and Peshawar changed hands intermittently between such rulers until early 11th century when Mahmud of Ghazni swept over the city, defeating the Hindu Shahi king Jayapaladeva at the Battle of Peshawar in 1001. For the next few centuries again Peshawar saw it being first ruled over by the Ghaznavids, who were overthrown by Muhammad Ghori in 1179-80; the city suffered attacks and destructions at the hands of the invading Mongols in 1200, after which mostly the Pashtun tribes again took over.

A consolidated rule over Peshawar was effected by the Mughals, with Babur taking the city in 1526 after defeating Daulat Khan Lodhi. Peshawar, in the Lodhi Empire was an important trade route, being situated at the eastern end of the famous Khyber Pass and was the gateway to the routes going to Central Asia. When Babur took over the city and made it his base, he changed the name of the city to *Begram*. It is important to note that till this time the city was called as *Parashawar*.

It was during the brief reign of the Afghan leader Sher Shah Suri, who ousted Humayun and took over his kingdom, that the construction of the famous *Grand Trunk Road* was started, in the 16th century. Peshawar was an important trading centre on the *Grand Trunk Road's* western end.

Peshawar under the later Mughals and after

Akbar renamed the city from Begram to Peshawar. The earlier name of *Parashawar* had been dropped and some historians say that while the new name Peshawar was well aligned with the city's older names of Purushapura and Parashawar, Akbar's chosen name Peshawar was derived from the Persian word *'pish-shehr'* meaning *'forward city'*. For the Mughals Peshawar was indeed a Frontier city.

Shah Jahan gave Peshawar its own set of *Shalimar Bagh* (gardens), but the same have been ruined and do not exist today. During Aurangzeb's rule, Peshawar was the winter capital for the Kabul province and the Mughal governor of Kabul, Mohabbat Khan, built the very famous *Mohabbat mosque* in the city. After Aurangzeb's death, as the Mughal power dwindled, they found it difficult to contain the tribes from attacking Peshawar. Finally in 1738, Peshawar was wrested from the Mughal Empire by the Persian king Nader Shah during his invasion of India.

For the next hundred years, from 1747 to 1839, Peshawar passed on respectively to first the Durranis from Afghanistan and then later the Sikhs under Maharaja Ranjit Singh. Many battles were fought for territorial supremacy in Peshawar and in the process the city suffered heavy damage and its bustling economy was busted.

Peshawar's importance in the British Raj era – The Durand Line

Following the second Anglo-Sikh war in 1839, most of the territories which were under the rule of the Sikhs were annexed and Peshawar too came under the British Raj rule. The city saw a period of stability as the British rebuilt a lot of infrastructure and restored many buildings which had been lying damaged since the previous wars. Railway connectivity was established to link Peshawar with the rest of British India. However, for the British, Peshawar was of significant importance as it was the closest inward frontier town from the north-western border of India. The British build large garrisons and established cantonments in Peshawar and it was from here that they officially marked out the demarcation line between India and Afghanistan and Persia.

Sir Mortimer Durand, a British diplomat and civil servant, and Abdur Rahman Khan, the Afghan Amir fixed their respective territories of influence and a Border was drawn between (undivided) India and Afghanistan in 1896, which was popularly called the *Durand Line*. The *Durand Line* cutting through the areas of the different Afghan-Pashtun tribes, scattered them on either side into the respective countries, causing much unrest and confusion among them. Peshawar was the city where the design and draft of the *Durand Line* was discussed and drawn by the British. In 1947, after independence, though Pakistan adopted the *Durand Line* as its western international border, it largely remained unrecognised by Afghanistan.

During the independence struggle, Peshawar was controlled by Khan Abdul Ghaffar Khan, a Pashtun activist who fought against the British rule. Ghaffar Khan was a devoted follower of Mahatma Gandhi and was nicknamed *'Frontier Gandhi'* by his people. He had rejected the proposal of the *All India Muslim League* for the creation of Pakistan and had opposed the *Indian National Congress* when they had agreed for the Partition of the country.

The modern era

The British had built a lot of buildings and had developed the city during their reign, much of which still stands today. Post partition, Peshawar became part of Pakistan and was made the capital of its *Khyber Pakhtunkhwa* province. The city had been the base for the CIA intelligence during the *Afghan-Soviet wars* in the 1980s. Like much of Pakistan's north-west frontier areas, Peshawar had also been severely affected during the *Taliban war* and continued subsequent violence by the *mujahiedeen* extremists in the Afghan refugee camps in and around the city. Arrival of large numbers of Afghan refugees into Peshawar has changed the character of the city to a great extent, in the present times.

However chequered the history of Peshawar may have been, the battle-scarred fate of the city continues even today as it stands vulnerable to the terrorist violence by radical and extremist groups operating around its Afghan border areas.

Qandahar

The city of Qandahar in present day Afghanistan is one of high cultural and historical significance, carrying a wealth of history and heritage. Qandahar's recorded history dates its origins to 329 BC and credits the foundation of the city to Alexander the Great, but an alternate mythological theory establishes that the city existed even during the *Mahabharata* times.

Etymology of Qandahar and the theories of its origins

The Mahabharata describes Qandahar as *Gandhara* ruled over by King Suvala and later by his son Shakuni. The princess of the *Gandhara* kingdom, Gandhari, was married to King Dhritarashtra of *Hastinapur*, an alliance formed by Bheeshma to forge matrimonial ties between the kingdoms of *Hastinapur* and *Gandhara*.

Gandhara in the early Vedic period was a Hindu-Buddhist kingdom located along the Kabul and Swat Rivers of Afghanistan and was famous for its wonderful climate, verdant settings and art, culture and learning. It was an expansive kingdom and included some significant ancient cities in it. Some historians are of the opinion that the name Qandahar has been derived from the *Gandhara* kingdom.

Many modern historians have associated the origins of Qandahar with Alexander the Great, who founded the city in 329 BC, while returning homewards after his aborted expedition of India. Alexander named the city *Alexandria in Arachosia*. Hence a theory has developed that the name Qandahar is a localised form of the name *'Iskander'* given to Alexander, *a.k.a Sikander,* in this part of the world.

However, as per later excavations done by the archaeologists like Louis Dupree in 1970, it was found that the Qandahar founded by Alexander was built on the ruins of a large fortified city which existed during the early 1st millennium BC. This proves the existence of the city in the days of the *Gandhara* kingdom and validates the description given in the *Mahabharata* about Qandahar.

The Buddhist heritage of Qandahar

Due to its strategic location and vantage point along the trade route connecting the Middle East and Central Asia to the Indian subcontinent, Qandahar was a hugely prosperous city and that made it always a target of conquest for different kingdoms who wanted to rule over the city. The region came under the *Seleucid Empire* after Alexander retreated, and then was ceded to the *Mauryan Empire* by way of a war-treaty. It was during the reign of the *Mauryas* and specifically Ashoka the Great that Buddhism was made the major religion and the region saw extensive installations of Buddhist sculptures, stupas, rock edicts and statues dotting its landscape. One of the major rock edicts of Ashoka which was later excavated read, *"Ten years of reign having been completed, King Ashoka made known the doctrine of Piety to men; and from this moment he has made men more pious, and everything thrives throughout the whole world."*

There is also evidence found that the city of Qandahar sent a delegation of thirty thousand Buddhist monks, led by a *'Mahadharmaraksita'* (the great preserver of *dharma*) to Sri Lanka for the dedication of the great Buddhist Stupa at *Anuradhapura*. That the region of *Gandhara* was predominantly Buddhist at the time of the *Mauryans*, is evident from the discovery of the mammoth Buddha statues at Bamyan (Sanskrit name: *Varmayana*). *[These were later destroyed by the Taliban extremists].*

Islamization of Qandahar

It was in the 7th century that different Arab armies started invading the region and converting the population to the new religion Islam. Yaqub ibn Layath Saffari of the *Saffarid* dynasty conquered Qandahar in 870 in the name of Islam. However, he could not consolidate his victory over the city as soon Qandahar was taken over by the *Hindu Shahi* kings of Kabul who ruled there till the 11th century when Mahmud of Ghazni attacked and pillaged the city. This was soon followed by the *Ghurids* from Ghor when they overthrew the *Ghaznavids* in the 12th century. By this time, Islam as the new religion had been consolidated in Qandahar and much of the earlier heritage had been destroyed in the wars.

Qandahar, over the next few centuries, exchanged hands between the *Mongols*, when Genghis Khan attacked the city in the 13th century and the *Timurids* (dynasty of Timur Lane) who ruled the city between the 14th and 15th centuries, before it was passed on to the *Arghuns* in the 15th century.

[Incidentally, it is said that the name Afghanistan was derived from the Arghun tribe who held sway over the place in the 15th century. The word Afghan was a localised corruption of the name Arghun.]

The famous historian Ibn Batuta, described Qandahar in 1333, as *"a large and prosperous town, three night's journey from Ghazni."*

Qandahar in the Mughal era

The *Mughal* affair with Qandahar began when Babur annexed the city in the 16th century. His son and successor Humayun lost Qandahar to the Persian *Safavids*, but Akbar managed to regain it in 1595. However, after Akbar's death in 1605, the *Safavids* once again attempted to recapture Qandahar but the Mughals led by Jahangir's generals laid siege to the city and successfully defended it. Between 1649 and 1653, the Mughals under Emperor Shah Jahan fought a sluggish war with the *Safavids* of Persia to retain their suzerainty over the cities of Qandahar, Badakshan and Balkh.

For the Mughals, retaining stronghold over the twin frontier cities of Kabul and Qandahar were important as they were the first point of defence against any invading Persian army. Further, Shah Jahan wished to extend the Mughal Empire all the way to *Samarkand,* the original home of the Mughals, wherefrom Babur had come, and thus undertook a concerted campaign with the assistance of his sons, Dara Shukoh, Aurangzeb and Murad Baksh. However, he met severe resistance from the Safavids in Qandahar and the Uzbeks in Balkh and could not advance further.

For four long years the battles continued in the North-west frontier of the Mughal Empire and fate played hide and seek with them as the cities of Qandahar and Balkh were captured and recaptured by the *Mughals* and *Safavids* by turns. This ambitious campaign was said to have put a huge strain on the Mughal exchequer and had cost the empire 20 million rupees. This was such a severe blow that even though in 1653, when the Mughals came out victorious in the war, Shah Jahan had to abandon the campaign and recall his troops. With the Mughal retreat, the *Safavids* promptly recaptured Qandahar and the city was lost to the Mughals forever.

Qandahar in later years

By the 1700s, Qandahar was being ruled over by the *Hotak dynasty* rulers, who were in constant skirmish with the *Durranis*. By 1738, the fearsome King of Persia, Nader Shah invaded Afghanistan and overthrew the *Hotak dynasty* and placed Ahmed Shah Durrani on the throne of Qandahar as a subjugate ruler to Persia, before proceeding on to attack the Mughal capital of Delhi. However, in 1747 after the death of Nader Shah, Ahmed Shah Durrani proclaimed independence and established the first true-blood Afghan rule and the *Durrani dynasty* in Qandahar, making the city the capital of his Afghan Empire. The Durranis expanded their empire to control the whole of Aghanistan, Pakistan, the Khorasan province of Iran and even parts of Punjab in India. Ahmed Shah's son and successor Timur Shah transferred the Afghan capital from Qandahar to Kabul in 1776.

The legend of the Kohinoor Diamond

It is said that after the death of Nader Shah, who looted the *Kohinoor* diamond among other valuables from the Mughal treasury in Delhi, his wealth was hastily divided and snatched away by his generals and family members. The *Kohinoor Diamond* remained with Nader Shah's grandson who later gave it to the Afghan king Ahmed Shah Durrani in return for his support during a battle in the Waziristan region.

While in possession of the Durranis, the home of the *Kohinoor Diamond* was Qandahar. Legend has it that in 1799, when Shah Zaman elder grandson and successor of the Durrani Empire was captured and blinded in a prison by rebel Afghan tribes, he hid his most precious ancestral gems, the *Kohinoor Diamond* and a *Pokhraj* in a crack of the prison wall. When his younger brother Shah Shuja successfully defeated the rebel tribe, avenged the blinding and murder of his brother and took over the Durrani throne in 1803, he set out in search of the two precious family gems. It is said that the *Kohinoor Diamond* was found to be with a *mullah* who was ignorantly using it as a paperweight, while the *Pokhraj* was found with a student. Needless to say, King Shuja Shah promptly acquired both the jewels.

When Maharaja Ranjit Singh gave shelter to Shuja Shah who had escaped to Lahore in 1813, leaving Qandahar in a state of civil war, Ranjit Singh extracted the Kohinoor

Diamond from him almost by force and torture, and thus the Kohinoor returned to India after the turn of almost a century.

Qandahar in later years, contd...

After the *Durrani Empire* disintegrated in 1813, entire Afghanistan was thrown into strife and civil war broke out between different Afghan tribes who fought for supremacy to rule the land. Qandahar passed through the hands of many such Afghan tribal chieftains and these wars ensured rapid deterioration of the city.

The British invaded Qandahar twice, leading their forces from India, first in 1839 during the *First Anglo-Afghan war*, but had to withdraw by 1842 after an unsuccessful campaign. They returned in 1878 and laid siege to Qandahar for almost three years, in what is known as the *Second Anglo-Afghan war*. Despite winning the Battle of Qandahar in 1881 and restoring stability to the city, the British forces had to retreat leaving the city in the hands of local Afghan rulers again.

For the next hundred years, Qandahar had a peaceful existence with different Afghan tribal chieftains succeeding each other and ruling over the city. It did not see much development but continued to be one of the important cities of Afghanistan.

The modern era

In the 1960s, Afghanistan was torn between United States of America and Soviet Russia, and while Russia made Kabul its war base, Qandahar became the base of the US armies. By 1980, the Soviet-backed Afghan government had taken control of Qandahar, but were harassed by the local *mujahideen* forces in ambush and guerrilla warfare. After the fall of the Afghan government led by *Najibullah* in 1992, the local *mujahideen* groups completely took over Qandahar which eventually led to the *Taliban movement* in 1994.

Qandahar was made the capital of their region by the *Taliban* and a stronghold militant base. It was during the *Taliban* regime in 1999 that an Indian Airlines plane was high-jacked and flown to Qandahar airport with its passengers held as hostage by a Pakistani extremist militant group. For the last 15 years or more, Qandahar has only seen insurgency and warfare between the NATO forces allied with the Afghan military and the insurgent *Taliban mujahideens* who have been joined and aided by different other extremist groups proclaiming jihad. Today, infamously Qandahar is known as the *'spiritual birthplace'* of the *Taliban* and remains one of the most insurgent regions of Afghanistan.

Rajouri

The picturesque town of Rajouri is located about 150 km from Jammu, on the *Poonch* highway. The place is known for its beautiful lakes and serene ambiance. It was this quaint town that was once the ancient capital of the Kamboja kingdom of the north-west, as early as the first millennium BC, when it was known as ***'Rajapura'***.

The Kamboja kingdom

The earliest references to the Kambojas are found in the Sanskrit grammarian *Panini's* works, in the 5th century BC. Even in the mythological texts such as the *Manusmriti* and *Mahabharata*, the Kambojas find mentions. They are described as *fallen Kshatriyas* (warriors) who were said to have degraded from their position due to failure to abide by Hindu sacred rituals. In the *Mahabharata,* there is a reference to *Karna* conducting an expedition against the Kambojas, at the behest of *Duryadhona,* the result of which was that the Kamboja tribe fought alongside the *Kauravas* in the *Kurukshetra* war. The later *Puranas* also mention the Kambojas as an *Uttarapatha* (North corridor) tribe who along with the *Sakas, Pahlavas, Barabaras* and *Yavanas* constituted the *Uttarapatha Pancha-gana* (five hordes of the North corridor).

Historical studies on the ethnicity of the Kambojas suggest that they were of *Indo-Iranian* race (sometimes referred to as *Indo-Aryans*) who had their territories beyond *Gandhara* - in modern day geography, beyond Afghanistan and lying in Tajikistan, Uzbekistan and Kyrgyzstan areas. During the *Mauryan* period, the Kambojas ruled independently and were friendly with the *Mauryans*. This is evidenced by the excavated Buddha statues, edicts and inscriptions of Ashoka regarding spread of Buddhism, found in the area.

By the *Maurya* period, the Kambojas had crossed over the Hindu-Kush range and entered *Gandhara* kingdom and settled in the region extending up to *Rajapura* (western face of Kashmir). The extent of the Kamboja kingdom, in this context, therefore ranged from the valley of Rajouri *(Rajapura)* in south-western Kashmir to the Hindu Kush range, with its borders extending probably as far as Kabul, Ghazni and Qandahar.

In *Sanskrit Puranic* literature, this region has been named as *'Komudha dvipa'* (the land of the *Komudhas*), while the Greeks referred to it as *'Komedes'* (ref.: geographical writings of Ptolemy). The Kambojas were also referred to as the *Ashvakas,* primarily because of their excellent breed of horses *(Sanskrit: Ashva)*. They had been referred to in the *Mahabharata* as *"ashva-yuddha-kushala"* (men expert in cavalry war).

In the Maurya period, Ashoka made a prominent mention of the Kambojas in his *Rock Edict no. XIII,* which described the Kambojas as *"araja vishaya"* meaning, kingless, which implied republican polities. In *Rock Edict no. V*, we find mention of Ashoka having sent Buddhist missionaries to the Kamboja land to convert the population to Buddhism.

Rajouri as the Kamboja capital

Kamboja was included and recognised as one of the 16 *Mahajanapadas* (kingdoms) in *Aryavarta* since the days of the *Mahabharata*. It had its capital in *Rajapura* (present day Rajouri). The *Mahabharata* mentions that Karna led an expedition to *Rajapura* just before the *Kurukshetra* war in order to gain their support for Duryodhana. In other references, especially in *Kautilya's 'Arthashastra'* and *Panini's 'Ashtadhyayi'*, Kamboja's capital is described as *Rajapura* which is the place of the King of Kamboja, who in turn is described as a *'titular head'* of a republican form of government. The line of Kamboja kings in Rajapura, as mentioned in the *Mahabharata* are *Chandravarmana Kamboja* (the first Kamboja king), *Kamatha Kamboja* and *Sudakshin Kamboja* who fought in the *Kurukshetra* war on the side of the *Kauravas* and were slain by *Arjuna*.

Rajouri in modern era

During the Sikh uprising of the early 1800s, Gulab Singh, a general of Maharaja Ranjit Singh of Lahore annexed Rajouri and made it a part of the Sikh Empire. Later, during British Raj, Gulab Singh was made the *Maharaja of Jammu and Kashmir* and Rajouri was ceded to him. Thus Rajouri became a part of Jammu and Kashmir and continued to stay so after Independence and partition.

However, in 1947-48 and in 1965, Rajouri was severely affected in the India-Pakistan wars, primarily because of its strategic location very close to the border. In 1965, during the Second Kashmir War, Rajouri was captured by the undercover Pakistani militia but later they withdrew their troops.

Rajouri today stands as a small town and municipal council, and home to some of the Kamboja ruins which remind visitors of its ancient history.

Sravasti

The city of Sravasti is one of the most important of India's ancient cities not only from a religious perspective, but also from that of learning, culture, architecture and art. Sravasti is famous for being the seat of Lord Buddha and the centre of entrenchment of Buddhism during the lifetime of the Buddha. However, Sravasti is an equally important centre for the Jains, as *Tirthankara Shambhavanath* was born there. Sravasti is located in the fertile Gangetic plains in present-day Uttar Pradesh and is 170 km north-east of Lucknow.

Mythological origins of Sravasti

In the *Ramayana*, Sravasti is mentioned as created as the capital city for Lav to rule over his part of the kingdom of Kosala, when Lord Rama divided his kingdom between his two sons. Lav ruled from Sravasti while Kush ruled from Kushavati. The *Mahabharata* states that Sravasti was named after the legendary king Sravasta of the *Suryavanshi* (Solar dynasty) lineage, who had founded the city. The city is situated on the banks of the Rapti River (then called *Achiravati*) and was a peaceful one with expansive agricultural tracts of land.

In the 6th century BC, King Prasenajit of the *Ikshvaku* clan (*Suryavanshi* line of Lord Rama) ruled over the region and had his capital at Sravasti. It was during the reign of King

Prasenajit that Lord Buddha arrived and started staying in Sravasti.

The treatise *'Brihatkalpa'* mentions that in the 14th century, this city was called *Maheth* and was a part of the twin establishment of *Saheth-Maheth* in the area. It is said that it is in the ruins found in *Maheth* that the ancient city of Shravasti stood. Excavations in the *Saheth-Maheth* region by Alexander Cunningham in 1863, have yielded sufficient evidences to validate this theory.

Buddha in Sravasti

Buddha came to Sravasti at the invitation of a merchant named Sudatta who had met him at *Rajagriha* (Rajgir), the capital of Magadha. Sudatta wished to build a monastery for Buddha in Sravasti and devoted all his wealth for that. The monastery was built on an expansive garden owned by King Prasenajit's son Jeta. Legend has it that Jeta asked Sudatta to cover the garden with gold as the price for purchasing the land, and when the devoted merchant painstakingly did so, the surprised Jeta had a change of heart and donated the wood of the trees in the garden to build the monastery. Thus the monastery came to be known as the *'Jetavana mahavihara'*. The other Buddhist monasteries in Shravasti were the *Pubbarama* and the *Rajakarama,* the latter being built by King Prasenajit himself.

Buddha stayed for 24 *Chaturmasas* (a holy period of four months in a year) in Sravasti, of which 19 were spent in *Jetavana* and the rest in *Pubbarama.* Buddha is said to have performed miracles in Sravasti, including the very famous *'twin miracle'* where simultaneously he had fire coming out of his shoulders and streams of water from his feet, thus representing the control of opposite elements of nature within his own self. A considerable amount of Buddha's preaching and sermons were delivered from Sravasti.

Later history of Sravasti

The later glorious period of Sravasti was during the rule of Emperor Ashok and then his grandson *Samrat* Samprati. Both of them upheld Buddhism in a glorious way and built a lot of Stupas and Buddhist temples in Sravasti.

The ancient city of Sravasti, which originally stood at the site of the twin establishments *Saheth-Maheth* saw decline since the 2nd and 3rd century. However, the modern Sravasti grew just on the outskirts of the ancient ruins and the settlement of its people gradually shifted to the new city.

The city is mentioned in the *'Brihatakalpa'* as a prosperous and prominent township in the Gupta period ($4^{th} – 5^{th}$ century AD). Chinese monks *Fa Hien* and *Hieuen Tsang* both of whom visited Sravasti (in different centuries) during their travels in India write about the city as a flourishing Buddhist habitation. Their accounts also mention about the ancient city in ruins, which however seemed to be well preserved and frequently visited by people.

However, by 900 AD, as the political scenario across the Gangetic plains of northern India changed and Kannauj assumed the imperial position as capital of an undivided Hindu India (northern region only), Sravasti came to be ruled by a dynasty of Jain kings. King Mayuradhwaj ruled over Sravasti in 900 AD, and is said to have also changed the name of the city to *'Manikapuri'*.

For the next one hundred years, the Jain kings Hansadhwaj, Makaradhwaj, Shudhavadhwaj and Suhridhwaj ruled over the city and the neighbouring region. This period marked the phenomenal rise of Jainism in Sravasti and the establishment of a number of Jain temples, thus making the city an important religious centre for the Jains.

King Suhridhwaj is credited with defending Sravasti and its temples against the invading Muslim forces in the early 11th century. However, by the 13th century, as the entire northern part of India was swamped by rapid Islamization, Sravasti was attacked and pillaged by Alauddin Khilji, who destroyed many temples and shrines in the city.

Sravasti does not offer an independent history of its own during the medieval period when India passed under the Muslim rulers of Delhi. The region was governed by the *subahdars* (governors) of the *Delhi Sultanate* kings and later the *Mughals*. During the reign of the *Nawabs of Awadh* and later the *British Raj*, Sravasti became a part of the majestic province of Awadh, however it continued to remain insignificant from a political or historical perspective.

Sravasti today

The sites of *Saheth* and *Maheth* are the location of the ancient Sravasti. *Maheth* was the city where people lived while *Saheth* was the location of the *Jetavana monastery*.

The walls of ancient Sravasti still stand and they encompass the ruins of the stupas of *Sudatta* (the merchant who originally invited Buddha to the city) and *Angulimala* (a fierce dacoit whom Buddha had converted to a monk). The stupa marking the site of Buddha's famous *'twin miracle'* is also located just outside the walls of the ancient city.

At *Saheth*, the ruins of *Jetavana monastery* can still be seen. It includes the *'Gandhakuti'* – Buddha's hut and abode in Sravasti where he spent for 25 rainy seasons, and the *Ananda-Bodhi* tree which is believed to have been planted by Sudatta after Buddha's arrival in Sravasti and under which Buddha preached. Buddhists consider the *Ananda-Bodhi* tree to be the second most sacred tree after the *Maha-Bodhi* tree in Bodh Gaya, under which Buddha attained enlightenment.

Takshashila

Takshashila is famous for being the first and earliest form of University in India. The city flourished as a seat of learning and trade and commerce under the early dynasties of rulers, but also declined rapidly and was ruined way too soon. Takshashila thus can be regarded as one of the earliest ancient cities of India.

Mythological origins and etymology of Takshashila

The *Ramayana* tells us that Bharata, brother of Lord Rama founded two cities in the *Uttarapath* (North corridor) region, viz., Pushkalavati and **Takshashila**, and installed his two sons Pushkala and Taksha to rule over them respectively. In *Sanskrit,* Takshashila is derived from *'Taksha'* and *'shila'* (rock), describing the foundation rock laid by Bharat's son Taksha for the city. In later *Pali* (Buddhist) language the city is called ***'Takkasila'*** while the Greeks referred to it as ***'Taxila'***, the name which has stuck to the city over the millennia down to the modern age. The *Ramayana* describes Takshashila as a magnificent city famous for its wealth and grandeur.

The *Mahabharata* refers to Takshashila as the place famous for two incidents. First, the *Kuru* kingdom's heir and grandson of Arjuna, Parikshit was enthroned at Takshashila. Second, it was at Takshashila that sage Vaisampayan (Rishi

Ved Vyas's pupil) recited the story of the *Mahabharata* to the later *Kuru* king Janmejaya, when was performing the snake-sacrifice. This was one of the first recitals of the Mahabharata and its audience included Ugrashravas, a travelling bard, who later disseminated the story to other people.

The Buddhist *Jataka* tales, especially the *Takshashila Jataka*, refer to the city as the capital of the *Gandhara* kingdom and describes it as a great seat of learning. It refers to many Buddhist monks being educated there and the glory of Buddhism in the region at that time.

History of Takshashila

The earliest history of Takshashila can be traced to around 3360 BC, based on the findings excavated in the region. However it is believed that the place was abandoned after the decline of the Indus valley civilization. The first major settlement at Takshashila commenced around 1000 BC. The region came within the eastern fringes of the **Achaemenid** and **Hellenistic** Empires, when they attacked the Indus valley region and held control over it for a few centuries. The Achaemenid rulers, King Daruis I and King Xerexes stationed their generals in the area who were tasked with exploring the Indus valley area.

Alexander the Great was able to take control of Takshashila in 326 BC without a fight. The city was meekly surrendered to him by King Ambhi (Greek: Omphis). The Greeks describe Takshashila as *"wealthy, prosperous and well-governed"*.

The city passed on to the **Mauryan Empire** when Chandragupta Maurya took control of it in 317 BC. His guide and advisor, Kautilya, is said to have taught at the Takshashila University and provided education to Chandragupta during which he spotted the spark in him worthy enough to form and rule an empire. Chandragupta Maurya made Takshashila into a regional capital and frontier town. During the *Maurya* period, Takshashila came to be located on the *'Royal Highway'* which connected the *Maurayan* capital Pataliputra (modern day Patna) to Purushapura (Peshawar), Pushkalavati (Gandhara) and onwards towards Central Asia via Kashmir, Bactria and Kapisa (Kabul region). This important location of Takshashila thus also made it an important centre for trade and commerce. During the time of Ashoka, Takshashila was turned into a great centre for Buddhist learning and a spring-board to spread Buddhism in the North-west region and beyond into Persia and Greece.

The next few centuries, the **Indo-Greeks, Indo-Scythians** and **Indo-Parthians** ruled over Takshashila and the region (in that order), until in the 1st century AD, the **Kushanas** took over the city. In the words of the Greek philosopher Apollonius who visited Takshashila around that time, the city was "fortified and well laid out. It was governed by King Kadphises..." (Said to be the founder of the Kushana Empire). The later powerful Kushana king, Kanishka, further glorified Takshashila by adding more Buddhist stupas and architecture to the place. He also patronised the Takshashila University and revived it.

By the 4th century AD, when the **Gupta Empire** held sway over entire Northern India, Takshashila was a city famous for its trade links. Trades in silk, sandalwood, horses, silverware, pearls and spices made it an oft visited city by travellers from Central Asia. Takshashila also featured prominently in the Classical Sanskrit literature which was at its zenith at the time, being referred to as both a centre of culture and learning as well as a militarised frontier town. The Chinese pilgrim *Fa Hien* visited Takshashila in 400 and describes the university in eloquent words.

Takshashila University

Though Takshashila is referred to as one of the earliest and ancient universities, the education system in Takshashila was quite far from that of a university. There were teachers in many disciplines, ranging across spirituality, medicine, economics, literature, mathematics, astronomy and the different sciences. The students used to come from different countries far and wide and would stay at the teachers' quarters till their studies were completed. There was no formal system of examination and the teacher would decide when a student was ready and had indeed understood the subject to his satisfaction. There were no formal education degrees conferred on the pass-outs of Takshashila either, as the knowledge gained was considered to be the reward in itself. Takshashila had an immense effect on Hindu culture and Sanskrit language from the ancient times.

Takshashila was famed for its eminent teachers and students. The foremost among them was **Chanakya,** also known as Kautilya, the eminent strategist who composed the

Arthashastra in Takshashila. The famous *Ayurvedic* healer, **Charaka** studied and perfected his skills in Takshashila. He also started teaching the science of medicine there at a later period. Another notable student-teacher of medicine at Takshashila was **Jivaka**, the court physician of King Bimbisara of Magadha, who had treated the Buddha in Pataliputra. The Kosala king, **Prasenajit** who patronised the Buddha at Sravasti during his time, was also a noteworthy student of Takshashila. **Panini,** the grammarian and expert of rhetoric, who codified the rules of Sanskrit grammar and language was a part of the community at Takshashila.

Decline of Takshashila

During the latter part of the Gupta period (450 AD), Takshashila fell in between the three-way war between the *Persians*, the *Kidarites* and the *White Huns* of western *Gandhara*. In the ensuing war in 470 AD, the White Huns swept over the *Gandhara* region including the city of Takshashila. Their barbaric warfare destroyed most of the Buddhist monasteries and stupas in the city and caused extensive damage to the living settlements thus completely disrupting the functioning of the university. By 540 AD, the Huns had completely taken over the region and were ruling in Takshashila, continuing sporadic devastation and damage. It was a blow from which the city could never recover.

On the religious front, *Vaishnavism* and *Shaivism* the important cults of Hinduism, began their resurgence after almost thousand years of Buddhist dominance. The ruling Huns took to *Shaivism* and began to promote the religion in the area, thus causing the Buddhist remnants of Takshashila to rapidly fall in decline. Hieuen Tsang, the much travelled Chinese monk who visited Takshashila in 630 AD, wrote that, *"most of the Buddhist sangharamas lay ruined and desolate and only a few monks remained there. The city had become a dependency of the Kashmir kingdom with local rulers fighting for its control..."*

Though Takshashila fell into decline and was completely ruined with subsequent disuse, it was around this time (7th century) that during some attacks on the city, some Brahmin priest-cum-scholars escaped and fled to the nearby *Kamboja kingdom* capital at Kabul. This refugee-delegation of Brahmins was led by a *jat-Brahmin* named Kallar who was well received and appointed as a minister in the *Turki-Shahi* court of Kabul. Kallar after sometime effected a successful coup against the ruling *Turki-Shahi* king and overthrew him to take the throne of Kabul for himself, thus establishing the *Brahmin Hindu-Shahi dynasty of Kabul*, one that he and his descendants ruled successfully for 300 years until Mahmud of Ghazni defeated and conquered them in the early 11th century.

The *Hindu-Shahis* of Kabul brought Takshashila and the entire region of *Gandhara* under their control during their reign, but by then Takshashila had been completely ruined and no efforts of revival were undertaken. Takshashila remained only in folklore, history and memories.

The Ruins of Takshashila

The lost city of Takshashila were not discovered until 1863-64, when Alexander Cunningham, the founder and first

Director-General of the Archaeological Society of India, mapped its location based on the notes left behind by the Chinese scholars Fa Hien and Hieuen Tsang. Among the major ruins at the site of Takshashila are the *Dharmarajika Stupa*, which houses the mortal remains (fragments of bones) of the Buddha; and the *Jaulian mahavihara* (site of the ancient Takshashila University).

It is believed that the *Dharmarajika Stupa* was first built on a grand scale by Emperor Ashoka, as a refurbishment of an earlier modest stupa housing Buddha's mortal remains. However, the stupa was damaged during later wars and was rebuilt to its current state by the *Kushana* king Kanishka in 2nd century AD.

The major sites of the ruins of Takshashila have been identified about 35 kms north-west of present-day Rawalpindi in Pakistan. It is accessible for visitors more easily from Islamabad by the direct motorway to Taxila. The site has now been named as an *UNESCO World Heritage Site* and also houses the Taxila Museum. Buddhist organisations in Thailand and Sri Lanka have been working together with the Archaeological department of Pakistan to revive and maintain the Buddhist relics and ruins in Takshashila.

Takshashila's ruins today feature as an important stop on the Buddhism pilgrimage circuit, which is famous as follows: Lumbini/Kapilavastu *(place of Buddha's birth)*, Bodh Gaya *(place of Buddha's enlightenment)*, Sarnath *(place where Buddha preached the first sermon - thus the founding of Buddhism)*, Sravasti *(place where Buddha performed miracles)*, and Taxila *(place where Buddha's mortal remains are held)*.

Ujjain

The city of Ujjain, located on the banks of the *Kshipra River* in present day Madhya Pradesh, has been an important centre for Hindu religious and cultural activities from the ancient times. The city has continued to thrive and prosper down the centuries and is now a bustling township in the central heartland of India.

Ujjain in the ancient times

The earliest settlements in Ujjain date back to 700 BC as per the excavated findings in the area. In ancient India, the kingdom was called *Avanti* with its capital at Ujjain. The city was also known as **Avantika** or **Ujjaini**. By 600 BC *Avanti* was one of the sixteen *Mahajanapadas* (kingdoms) of *Aryavarta* (north India), the references of which we find in many ancient texts like the *Puranas*. Ujjain as the capital and a prominent city on the *Malwa* plateau, remained as an important political, commercial and cultural centre.

The people of Ujjain celebrated Lord Shiva as their guiding deity and devotedly worshipped him. Mythology has it that Lord Shiva impressed with the devotion of the people, granted their wish and resided in the city in his form of *'Mahakaleshwar'* – the fiery column of light which signified the unending passage of time. A large and ornate temple was built in 600 BC to worship Lord Shiva in the *Mahakaleshwar* form in Ujjain, which is one of the holiest and most visited Shiva temples in India. The temple stands till date and is held as a place of pilgrimage by devout Hindus.

Ujjain flourished greatly during the *Mauryan* period. Ashoka was first the viceroy of *Avanti* when his father Bindusara ruled the empire and later when he became the Emperor, he glorified Ujjain to a large extent. After the *Mauryans,* Ujjain was ruled over by local rulers like the *Shungas* and the *Satvahanas* until the Gupta period of history.

During the *Gupta era*, entire north India saw a revival of *Classical Hinduism* and resurgence of *Sanskrit* language. Ujjain emerged as a notable centre for intellectual learning for Hindu, Buddhist and Jain texts and literature as well as art and architecture. The celebrated poet Kalidasa eloquently described the city of Ujjain and its people in his fine composition *Meghaduta*. Bhartrihari composed his great epics *Virat Katha* and *Neeti Sataka*, where the love story of princess Vasavadatta and Udayan was set in the city of Ujjain. The famous literary composition *Mrichchakatika* by Sudraka was based in Ujjain as were many of Bhasa's works. Ujjain also appears as the capital of the legendary King Vikramaditya during this period. Composed in the later Gupta period (10th century), Somadeva's *'Kathasaritsagara'* describes Ujjain as *"a city built by Vishwakarma and being invincible, prosperous and full of wonderful sights."*

Ujjain in the medieval to modern period

During the rapid conquest of northern India by the *Delhi Sultanate* kings, Ujjain was attacked by Sultan Iltutmish in 1234. The city was pillaged and plundered and the centuries-old *Mahakaleshwar Shiva* temple was severely damaged. This attack on the city was a huge setback from which the city could only recover much later. For the ensuing centuries as the country passed through the Muslim rule from Delhi Sultanate till the *Mughals,* Ujjain remained a low profile centre. However it was still venerated as an important pilgrimage place by the Hindus who flocked there.

By the early 18th century when the Mughal power in Delhi was waning and most of the kingdoms in India had asserted their independence, Ujjain came to be ruled over by the *Maratha Scindia dynasty*. However, the Scindias soon shifted their base to Gwalior from where they continued to rule. In 1736, the Maratha general Ranoji Scindia rebuilt the *Mahakaleshwar Shiva temple* (to its present structure) in Ujjain and restored its earlier reverence and architectural grandeur to a great extent.

The *Scindias* and the *Holkars* of the region continuously fought for the suzerainty of Ujjain until both were subdued by the advancing British armies. As Ujjain and the region passed under the *British Raj*, they decided to reduce the importance of Ujjain and promote Indore as the alternate power centre for the region. This had also to do with the merchants of Ujjain refusing to support the British policies, and their direct revolt towards the British motives.

After Independence, Ujjain continued to be part of Madhya Bharat region until 1956 when it was infused into the state of Madhya Pradesh.

Ujjain is considered to be one of the seven holy cities for the Hindus *(Sapt-puri)* and a major pilgrimage centre. It is also the venue of the *Kumbh-mela* - the religious fair which occurs once every 12 years on the banks of the *Kshipra River*, the last one being held in 2016. Ujjain recently has also been selected under the *'Smart City Development Programme'* by the Government of India.

Varanasi

Mark Twain, being enthralled by the legend and sanctity about Benaras once said: *"Benaras is older than history, older than tradition, older even than legend and looks twice as old as all of them put together."* Thus to gauge and fathom the legend of Benaras in itself is an awe-inspiring and mammoth task. There are innumerable legends, myths and tales surrounding Benaras, spread across many ancient texts, mythology and historical accounts, in both Hinduism and Buddhism as it is across different eras of Indian history.

The Legend of Varanasi's origin and its etymology

Varanasi or ***Benaras*** was known as ***Kashi*** in the ancient texts and mythological tales. In Sanskrit, Kashi means *'the city of Shining Light'*, an epithet that the city has truly lived up to, being a luminous centre of religion and learning from time immemorial. The name Varanasi comes from the city's location, being based at the confluence of two of Ganga's tributary rivers, *Varuna* and *Assi*. The name is therefore attributed to these rivers: the *Varuna* still flows as a channel in the northern part of Varanasi, while the extinct *Assi* River is remembered by the famous *Assi ghat* in Varanasi on the Ganges.

Varanasi or Kashi is believed to be the *'city of Lord Shiva'*. The ascetic that he was, Shiva decided to settle down in the plains (leaving his Himalayan abode) after his marriage to Parvati, and chose Kashi as his new home. Shiva therefore is known and worshipped as *'Kashi Vishwanath'* (the Lord of the world in Kashi) in Varanasi.

The legend of King Divodasa who with the boon of Brahma established the utopian rule of the *'Dharma'* in Varanasi and consequently banished Lord Shiva and all other Gods from the city, is very popular in mythology. Lord Vishnu finally managed to skilfully depose the righteous king Divodasa and return the city of Varanasi to Lord Shiva.

The oldest archaeological evidences found from the region of Varanasi dates back to about 1000 BC, but mythological references to Kashi take us back much earlier. The *Mahabharata* mentions that the *Pandavas* came to Kashi in search of Lord Shiva to atone for their sins of fratricide and *Brahmanhatya* (killing of Brahmins) which they had committed during the *Kurukshetra* war. Kashi is considered as one of the seven holy cities as per Hindu beliefs, along with Ayodhya, Avanti, Mathura, Hardwar, Kanchi and Dwarka.

Varanasi as a centre of religion and learning

The city over the eras has emerged as a prominent centre of religious exuberance and entrenched learning. Lord Buddha is said to have founded Buddhism in Varanasi in 528 BC when he delivered his first sermon *"The Setting in motion of the Wheel of Dharma"* at the nearby location of Sarnath. The Chinese monk and pilgrim Hieuen Tsang wrote about Varanasi when he visited the city in 635 BC, *"a centre of religious and artistic activities..."* He referred to Varanasi as *'Polonisse'* in his accounts.

In the 8th century *Adi Shankaracharya* established Shaivisim, the cult of Shiva, as the official sect for Varanasi, adding to the religious prominence of the city. Varanasi's religious importance and celebration of Hindu culture continued even through the medieval period when India came under the dominance of Muslim rule. *Tulsidas* composed the *Ram Charita Manas* in Varanasi, and several luminaries of the *Bhakti movement*, viz., *Kabir* and *Ravidas*, were born here. An important *Maha-Shivratri* festival was hosted in Varanasi in 1507 which is said to have been attended by *Guru Nanak*, which gave an impetus to the founding of *Sikhism* as a new religion.

At the same time, Varanasi also suffered heavily during the invasions by Muslim armies, viz., Mahmud of Ghazni and Muhammad Ghori who destroyed and looted many temples in the city and killed and enslaved many of its people. Also during the reign of different Muslim dynasties of the Delhi Sultanate, Varanasi was often attacked and ransacked by the invading armies. Such frequent attacks and plundering gave temporary setbacks to the city and its spirit of culture and learning.

Later history of Varanasi

During the reign of Mughal Emperor Akbar, Varanasi experienced a revival of Hindu culture and religion. Akbar invested in the city and built two large temples dedicated to *Shiva* and *Vishnu*, while other kings also contributed to building and restoring temples and promoting classical Hindu learning in Varanasi. The city saw another setback and lull during the reign of Aurangzeb who ordered the destruction of many temples and imposed restrictions on religious practices of the non-Muslims.

However, by 1737 the Mughals accorded official status to the Kingdom of Benaras under the ruling of the *'Kashi Naresh'* (king of Kashi). Much of the modern Varanasi was built and developed by the *Maratha* and *Brahmin* rulers in the 18th century. Maharaja Ranjit Singh of Lahore and of the Sikh confederacy fame got the tower of the *Kashi Vishwanath* temple gilded in gold leaves. The sanctity of Varanasi continued during the *British Raj* with the British establishing colleges and modern institutions of education and learning. The *Sanskrit College of Benaras*, founded in 1791 by Jonathan Duncan was foremost among such institutions. The *Central Hindu College* founded by Dr Annie Besant later became the foundation of the creation of the *Benaras Hindu University*.

While the British technically ruled over the region and also transferred the capital of the Kingdom of Benaras to Ramnagar, across the Ganges, the *'Kashi Naresh'* continued to remain the religious head of Varanasi and was much revered by its people.

The epitome of Varanasi

While Varanasi continues to be the cultural capital of North India since a long time, the epitome of its fame lies in its close association with the *Ganga* River on the banks of which the city is situated. The *'ghats'* (embankment of stone steps going down to the river) of Varanasi are world famous, with the *'Dashashwamedh Ghat'* being the most popular of them all. Other important *'ghats'* are *Panchganga ghat, Assi ghat, Manikarnika ghat* and *Harishchandra ghat;* the latter two being where Hindus cremate their dead. It is a popular belief amongst Hindus that death in the city will wash away all earthly sins and bring salvation *(moksha).*

Varanasi also remains as an important centre for culture and music and is the place where the *'Benaras gharana'* form of *Hindustani Classical Music* was developed.

Waihind

The town of Waihind has been known in history by different name variants, as it has been held in importance by significant events which have changed the course of history a few times. Albeit an ancient small town, and now almost a hamlet, the history of Waihind cannot be ignored when we talk about ancient and medieval periods of undivided India. The primary reason for its importance has always been the strategic location. Situated on the right (west) bank of the Indus River, about 15 km from present-day Attock and 80 km east from Peshawar, in the Swabi district of modern Pakistan, Waihind has always been the preferred point of crossing the Indus River and entry into Hindustan for every traveller from the west.

Importance of Waihind in ancient times

References to **Waihind** are found in the 12th century poet Kalhana's *'Rajatarangini'* (History of Kashmir), wherein the town is referred to as *Udakabanda*, which could be a colloquial shortening or derivative of the Sanskrit term *'Urdhva-banda'*, meaning 'an upper town' *[In Sanskrit: Urdhva means Upper and Bhianda means Town; the word 'banda' most likely is a derivative of 'Bhianda'.]* Some other texts of the time refer to the town as *'Udabhandapura'* which is yet another derivative of the same name. During the ancient period of the 8th to 11th century, the place was more popularly called Waihind, which later on got corrupted to ***Ohind*** and finally came to rest as ***Hund***, the name with which we know it in the present day.

Waihind was the site of Alexander the Great's crossing of the Indus and entering India, as it was centuries later for all the other invaders from the west, viz., the Scythians, Kushanas, Mahmud of Ghazni, Muhammad Ghori, Babur and also the Chinese pilgrims who came to India via the Hindu-Kush route, all crossed the Indus River at Waihind to enter the plains of India.

During the 2nd century, the city was made a part of the Kushana empire spanning entire *Gandhara* region with the capital at *Purushapura* (ancient Peshawar). From the excavation findings in the area, it is seen that the Kushanas built settlements, houses, and gateways and planned streets in Waihind. Around the 7th century till the 11th century, Waihind and the entire *Gandhara* region were a part of the *Hindu Shahi* Empire being ruled from Kabul. After the *Hindu Shahi* kings, Jayapala and his son Anandapala were defeated in Kabul and Peshawar, their first and second capital cities, the *Hindu Shahi* dynasty moved their capital to Waihind and ruled their empire, albeit reduced in territory, from the city.

However, the status of Waihind as the capital of *Gandhara* under the *Hindu Shahi* kings was short-lived as Mahmud of Ghazni defeated King Jayapala in the *First Battle of Waihind* in 1001 and his son Anandapala in the *Second Battle of Waihind* in 1008, thus pillaging and destroying Waihind considerably. The *Hindu Shahi* king, Anandapala ceded Waihind to the *Ghaznavid Empire* and moved his capital to a new location Nandana in the Salt Range Mountains. Waihind lived on as an eastern frontier town of the *Ghaznavid Empire* but lost all its glory, status and economic prosperity forever.

References of Waihind in earlier texts

Kalhana in his *Rajatarangini* described Waihind as *"to the North of the Indus, there is a city of complete merit by name Udabhanda where communities have made their home ... protected by the chief of kings Bhima of terrible valour by whom the earth was protected... It is a place where kings ousted from their own territories by enemies, found safety... "*

By the last line, it is supposed that Kalhana was referring to the ousting of the *Hindu Shahi* kings by Mahmud of Ghazni in 1001, and the shifting of their capital to Waihind.

According to the *Hudud al-Alam*, an anonymous tenth century work, Waihind was a large town and received merchandize such as musk and other precious stuffs. It served as a trade centre between India and Central Asia. An eminent Muslim writer of the time, Maqadsi describes Waihand, *"with its fine gardens, numerous streams, abundant rainfall, good fruits, cheap prices and general prosperity of its people. On the outskirts of the city were walnut and almond trees and within it bananas and the like. The houses were made of wood and dressed stone. The city itself was greater in size than Mansura (Sind)... "*

Waihind in the medieval and modern periods

Waihind was included as a part of the *Delhi Sultanate* and was ruled over by different generals under the dynasties that took the throne at Delhi by succession. However, the town had reduced considerably in its political significance by then and remained important only as the point of crossing the Indus.

Understanding the strategic importance of Waihind and a cross-over point on the Indus, *Mughal Emperor* Akbar ordered the construction of a large fort on the mounds of the place. However, the final nail to the importance of Waihind was also driven in during the reign of Emperor Akbar. The final construction and formation of the Grand Trunk Road (it was named so later by the British) and the building of massive bridges at Attock to easily cross over the Indus River, robbed Waihind of all its traffic, travellers and commercial activity related to the travel route from which it had benefitted so long. Waihind thus continued to languish and was relegated into insignificance.

Post the decline of the *Mughal Empire*, and with no focus whatsoever on Waihind, the city became part of the disintegrated smaller kingdoms held by different regional tribes. The notable among them were the *Khans* and *Mians* who mixed with the families of *Balar Khel* and *Habib Khel* in the region to establish their control. The name of Waihind had also changed to **Hund** by then, primarily under colloquial reference and influence. Their most popular ruler was Khadi Khan.

As the *British* took over the entire region, the chieftain of the *Balar Khel* village of Waihind, Khan Bahadur Khan joined hands with the British forces to fight against the advancing Maratha armies. Post these wars, Waihind came fully under the control of British territory and the land was snatched from the local *Khan* rulers.

After independence and the creation of Pakistan, the city continues with the name Hund and also houses the *Hund Museum* which stores the artefacts found in different excavations conducted in the area. The Mughal Fort built by Akbar right across the village, still stands, but in considerable ruin.

In the words of Dr Ahmed Hasan Dani, a chronicler of the *Gandhara* civilization, *(in an interview to The Express Tribune, Pakistan)… "It is often said that history repeats itself and present day Hund is a testimony to this fact. From the courtyard of the Hund Museum, one can see vehicles crossing the Peshawar-Islamabad Motorway Bridge over the River Indus in the winter haze. It was in 1586 when Akbar built the Attock bridge-crossing on the River Indus… The construction of Grand Trunk Road and the Attock bridge-crossing had pushed Hund into oblivion. Today, the new motorway bridge signifies that history is retracing its steps to Hund…"*

Xuanzang

Xuanzang is the historic Chinese pilgrim and Buddhist monk who came to India in the 7th century to study and acquire knowledge on the core tenets of Buddhism. Xuanzang was known by a few name variations in his birth land China and was known in India by the name of **Hieuen Tsang.**

He is famous for not only having travelled throughout the expanse of India but also for the closely detailed accounts of his travels that he has left behind. These notes and accounts have been invaluable in establishing details about many of India's ancient cities when the later historians and archaeologists set out to identify and record the history of these cities.

Hieuen Tsang's notes helped not only to reveal locations of lost ancient cities, but also gave us sufficient glimpses of the life in India's ancient cities in his time. We come to know about religion, kings, culture, art and architecture, literature and language, administration and even earlier history of many of our ancient cities through Hieuen Tsang's descriptions.

It is only fitting and necessary that while on the theme of *Ancient Cities of India*, we take a look into the life of Hieuen Tsang and his expansive travels across many ancient cities of India.

Hieuen Tsang's early life

Hieuen Tsang was born in 602 AD in the Henan province of China and from his boyhood days itself was drawn to reading religious books and stories of ancient sages. Though his family followed the religion of *Confucius*, he followed in the footsteps of his elder brother and took a deep interest in Buddhism. He was ordained as a Buddhist monk at the age of twenty and by then had travelled to many cities in China in search of Buddhist books and treatises.

Hieuen Tsang was most moved by the incompleteness and differences he saw in Chinese Buddhism and what he learnt of Indian Buddhism at that time. When he no longer found answers to his questions in China, he decided to visit India and the Central Asia regions where Buddhism had spread, to learn the Indian Buddhism doctrines right in the cradle of the religion and in the land of the Buddha himself.

Hieuen Tsang knew about *Faxian's* (*Fa Hien* – another Buddhist monk and traveller who had visited India in the 4th century) travel to India and like him was confused with the misinterpreted nature of the Buddhist books that had reached China. Having decided to undertake the travel to India, Hieuen Tsang learnt *Sanskrit* and also took interest in the metaphysical *Yogacara* school of Buddhism. Accordingly he left his homeland in 629 AD and started the long and arduous journey to India in the quest of knowledge of the true doctrines and practices of Buddhism.

Hieuen Tsang's route to India

Upon leaving his province in China, Hieuen Tsang travelled across the Gobi Desert to reach **Hami** city (in Xinjian area of China), there onwards following the *Tian Shan* mountain range westwards to reach **Turpan** in 630 AD. He travelled further west and crossed the *Bedel Pass* and entered *Kyrgyzstan*, where he toured a few monasteries of the *Mahayana* Buddhist school. Continuing further, he visited **Tashkent** and **Samarkand** (in present day Uzbekistan) and impressed the ruling Persian king with his preaching. He also visited the abandoned Buddhist monasteries and relics in these cities. Moving southwards and crossing the *Pamir* mountain range and passing through the famous *Iron Gates*, he reached *Amu Darya* and the city of **Termez** where he met a large congregation of Buddhist monks. Their abbot *Dharmasimha* advised Hieuen Tsang to visit **Balkh** in Afghanistan and see the Buddhist sites and relics at the *Nava vihara*. It was here that Hieuen Tsang met another notable Buddhist monk *Prajnakara* with whom he stayed and studied the scriptures for some time. Together they travelled to **Bamyan** where they saw the two mammoth and magnificent Buddha statues carved out of the rock-face.

Hieuen Tsang then crossed over through the *Shibar Pass* and reached **Kapisa**, in the **Kabul** region, which had 100 *Mahayana* Buddhist monasteries and more than 6000 monks. Hieuen Tsang participated in religious debates here and engaged other monks on his discourses on the various schools of Buddhism. It was here that he first met the first *Hindus* and *Jains* of his journey. Towards the end of 630,

Hieuen Tsang reached **Adinapur** (modern day **Jalalabad** in Afghanistan) where he thought that he had reached India.

Hieuen Tsang's travels in India

From **Adinapur**, Hieuen Tsang crossed the *Khyber Pass* and reached **Purushapura,** (ancient Peshawar) the earlier capital of the *Gandhara* kingdom. Buddhism was on the decline in **Peshawar** at that time but had an immense wealth of ruined monasteries and stupas. The most notable of them was the *Kanishka stupa* which Hieuen Tsang described in his accounts. Much later, in 1908, the *Kanishka stupa* was rediscovered by archaeologist D B Spooner with the help of Hieuen Tsang's records.

Hieuen Tsang then travelled further east and crossed the Indus River at **Waihind** (modern day **Hund** in Pakistan) and moved on to **Takshashila**. Takshashila had been a very famous centre of learning especially for Buddhism in the latter years, but by the time Hieuen Tsang reached there the place had been ruined. He laments in his travel account of Takshashila, *"the place is ruined and desolate though some monks continue to live on... the city is now a dependency of Kashmir, though once it was a part of the Kapisa (Kabul-Gandhara Empire)."*

Hieuen Tsang met a very talented Buddhist monk *Samghayasas* in **Kashmir** in 631 AD and with him visited many monasteries in the region. Between 632 and 633, he spent 14 months visiting about 100 monasteries and interacting with many monks and studying early scriptures of Buddhism under the well-known monks *Vinitprabha* and

Chandravarman. He also visited **Lahore** during this time along with other cities in the region. His accounts also give us the earlier history of these ancient cities alongside the description of life during the time of his visit.

In 634, Hieuen Tsang arrived in **Jalandhar**, before entering the **Kullu** *valley* where he visited the *non-Mahayana* Buddhist monasteries to study their doctrines. He turned southward and then visited **Bairat**, another important Buddhist monastery location, and then finally traversed up the *Yamuna River* to reach **Mathura**. Though a Hindu-dominated place, Mathura had 2000 monks from both the *Hinayana* and *Mahayana* faiths of Buddhism. Having visited many monasteries which dotted the region, Hieuen Tsang then crossed the *Ganges River* and reached **Kannauj** the capital of King Harsha's empire at that time.

Hieuen Tsang was completely overawed by King Harsha's grand capital and the peaceful co-existence of religions in the region. King Harsha played an excellent host and installed Hieuen Tsang with great honour in his court. Religious debates and discourses flowed and Hieuen Tsang continued to visit monasteries in the region. He found a wealth of information to study, not only in Buddhism alone, but also gaining knowledge of Hinduism, reading many texts composed in Sanskrit and taking a taste of classical and religious literature. He continued to stay on in **Kannauj** under the patronage of King Harsha and records state that he visited few hundred monasteries and interacted with the monks there. He writes that he was greatly impressed by the King's patronage of both scholarship and Buddhism.

Hieuen Tsang next visited **Ayodhya** in 636 AD, which was the homeland of the metaphysical *Yogacara* school of Buddhism. Over the next year, he travelled to **Kaushambi** (near **Allahabad**), **Sravasti, Kapilavastu** in Nepal and finally reached **Lumbini**, Buddha's birthplace. In 637, he started his travel again and visited **Kusinagara** (the place of Buddha's death) and moved on to visit **Varanasi** and **Sarnath** (the founding seat of Buddhism) and further making stops at **Vaishali** (north Bihar), **Pataliputra** (modern **Patna**) and **Bodh Gaya**. From there the local monks took Hieuen Tsang to **Nalanda** where the *Mahavihara* (university) was fully functioning at that time.

Hieuen Tsang stayed on in *Nalanda University*, enrolling as a student under the tutelage of the very famous Buddhist monk *Silabhadra*. He studied logic, grammar, Sanskrit and the *Yogacara* school of Buddhism during his time in **Nalanda**. The venerable *Silabhadra* was the superior of the *Nalanda Mahavihara* at that time and his association with Hieuen Tsang became legendary. Rene Grousset, the French historian specializing on Oriental history, writes, *"The Chinese pilgrim had finally found the omniscient master, the incomparable metaphysician who was to make known to him the ultimate secrets of the idealist systems... Silabhadra had been trained by the founders of Mahayana idealism, and was thus in a position to make available to the world the entire heritage of Buddhist idealism. The "Siddhi", Xuanzang's great philosophical treatise... is none other than the summary of this doctrine, the fruit of seven centuries of Indian Buddhist thought."*

From **Nalanda**, Hieuen Tsang travelled on to the Eastern kingdoms of India and visited notable monasteries at

Tamralipta (**Tamluk** in West Bengal), **Sylhet** (in present Bangladesh) and **Pragjyotishpura** in Kamarupa (modern day **Guwahati** in Assam) before treading on to South India where he visited the monasteries at **Kanchi** (Kanchipuram) amongst other cities. Across the Deccan, Hieuen Tsang also visited **Nashik, Ajanta** and **Ujjain** before proceeding northwards onto **Multan**.

In 643 AD, Harsha invited Hieuen Tsang back to **Kannauj** where he had organised a great Religious Assembly. This was followed in the same year by another Religious Assembly at **Prayag** (Allahabad), which was titled the *'Mahamoksha Parishad'*. Glorious descriptions of both the Assemblies are given in Hieuen Tsang's accounts. Harsha had made Hieuen Tsang the *Chief Guest* of the Assemblies and honoured him with the title of *"Master of the Law"*. These religious assemblies were attended by many neighbour kings and large congregations of Hindu Brahmins and Buddhist monks. Hieuen Tsang was greatly impressed by the magnanimity of King Harsha towards all religions and his generosity towards his subjects. *"History does not present another example of a king who gave away his wealth so freely to the believers and the needy, as did this king..."* Hieuen Tsang wrote about King Harsha at the end of the Religious Assemblies.

Hieuen Tsang's return to China

Hieuen Tsang was given a grand farewell by King Harsha in 645 AD in Kannauj and he set out laden with a caravan full of gifts and accompaniments. He travelled through the

Khyber Pass of the Hindu Kush Mountains and reached China, sixteen years after he had left his homeland. His return was greatly celebrated by the Chinese Emperor *Taizong of Tang* who offered him special appointments in his empire. But Hieuen Tsang declined such appointments and instead retired to a monastery where he spent time in translating Buddhist scriptures and texts and assimilating his travel accounts. It is said that he returned with over 600 *Mahayana* and *Hinayana* Buddhist texts, 7 statues of the Buddha and over 100 relics. Hieuen Tsang passed away in 664 AD, leaving behind a wealth of information.

While his main purpose was to receive Buddhist scriptural knowledge, texts and instructions on Buddhism while he was in India, he had indeed done and left back much more. He had preserved the records of all political and social aspects of the cities and lands he visited and such chronicles have immensely helped later historians to reconstruct the history of the 7th century India and throw valuable light on the history of its ancient cities.

The *Xuanzang Memorial Hall* in Nalanda has been constructed in memory of this great Chinese pilgrim and Buddhist monk.

Yavana

References to the *'Yavanas'* are abound in various texts and literature of ancient India. From the *Ramayana* to the *Mahabharata*, the *Puranas* and later Buddhist and classical *Sanskrit* compositions, all have referred to the *'Yavanas'* over the ages. However, it is interesting that the *'Yavanas'* have always been portrayed as the enemies of the *'Aryavarta'* kingdoms. Mythology refers to the *'Yavanas'* as a tribe residing in the further western sphere beyond the reach of the Indian kingdoms, while later history refers to them as barbaric people of foreign origin who are uncouth in their ways, speak an incomprehensible language and are unruly in their behaviour.

Thus far, in this selection of *Ancient Cities of India*, we have seen glorified kingdoms, imperial cities, exemplary rulers and magnificent cities. As we draw to the end of the series, it would certainly be interesting to know about the *'Yavanas'*, who were considered the enemies of ancient Indian kingdoms. Were they truly enemies of the ancient Indian kingdoms and caused damage and destruction, or were they just another race of people whom the ancient Indians failed to comprehend? Mythology and history have many theories and counter-theories on the subject, but we will attempt to understand the most logical of them.

Etymology of the 'Yavanas'

The usage of the term *'Yavana'* has been particularly linked with the Greeks and *'Yavana kingdom'* with the Greek kingdoms which neighboured and sometimes occupied territories of the north-western region of ancient India.

The Greeks are known to have worshipped *Ion*, the son of Apollo. Ion was once a peaceful worshipper at Delphi but later turned into a warlord and won great battles. The Greek tribe of *Ionians* who resided in the (ancient) kingdom of *Ionia* were famous as the Eastern Greeks. Ionia was the region of Anatolia in present day eastern Turkey. The Ionians were always in strife with the Persians who were their neighbours. Many of the Ionian Greeks migrated further east and came to reside in the north-western region of ancient India. The Ionians thus had interactions and often wars with the ancient Indian kingdoms.

The terms *'Yona'* and *'Yavana'* are transliterations of the Greek word *'Ionian'* in *Pali* and *Sanskrit* respectively, and were the first Greeks to be known in the East. This theory has been established in many ancient mythological and historical texts in India. Thus we may understand that *'Yavana'* originally meant and referred to the Greeks who settled in their tribes in the north-western neighbourhood of ancient India.

It is interesting to note that the Eastern Greeks were referred to by similar sounding names by other races of people as well. The Egyptians called them *'j-w-n-n'* while the Assyrians referred to them as *Iawanu*. The Persians called them *Yaunas* while the Babylonians called them *Yaman* or *Yamanaya*. In Biblical Hebrew, the Greeks are called *Yavan*, while in Arabic they are referred to as *Yunan*. In Indian Sanskrit they are called the *'Yavana'* tribe.

References to Yavanas in ancient India

The *Mahabharata* classifies the *Yavanas* with other tribes who stayed *'beyond Uttarpatha'*, viz., the *Kambojas* (Indo-Iranians), *Pahlavas* (Parthians), *Shakas*, and *Bahlikas*. The *Yavanas* were the Greeks and the Indo-Greeks. Their kingdoms were situated beyond *Gandhara*, which was considered to be the outer-limit of the north-western frontier. These five tribes together were called the *'Mlechchas'* in ancient Hindu terminology, meaning people of foreign extraction.

We also find references of *'Yavana'* invasion of *Majjhidesa* (central India of the time) mentioned in the *Mahabharata*. Ancient texts also cite strong prophesies and warnings against wars and destruction to be caused to Indian cities and traditions by the *'Yavanas'* and *'Mlechchas'* in due course of time in the *Kaliyug*.

Buddhist texts of 2nd century BC and later also cite strong references and mentions of *Yavanas*. The *Dipavamsa, Mahavamsa* and *Milindapanha,* all mention detailed interaction with the Greek kings and subjects while spreading Buddhism. The *Greco-Buddhist monasticism* is also said to have taken shape during this period. Tales of the *Yona* (Greek) monk *Dharmarakshita* are also found in detail in the Buddhist texts written in *Pali* language.

During the rule of Emperor Ashoka (250 BC), his Rock Edict nos. V and XIII found in ancient *Gandhara* region, mention the *Yonas* along with *Gandhara* and *Kamboja* people as his subjects in the frontier towns of the north-west. The inscriptions also attest that Ashoka had regular links with the Greek kings of the west and sent emissaries to their courts. *"Amtiyoko nama Yonaraja...* (The Greek king by the name of Antiochus)" quotes one inscription, which unambiguously establishes *Yonas* as the Greeks.

Gradual expansion of the term 'Yavanas'

With time, the term *'Yavana'* began to acquire a much broader meaning and scope. While the Greeks left the neighbouring kingdoms of the north-western border and retreated, interaction with them also diminished. Their erstwhile kingdoms came to be occupied by newer tribes who still remained foreign to the Indian kingdoms. The term *'Yavana'* therefore stuck to them and grew to include in its meaning and reference, people of foreign origin with a different language and way of life. As most of the tribes occupying that region continued to have wars and skirmishes with the Indian kingdoms, their behaviour were always referred to as barbaric and damaging.

Thus by the 3rd century AD, the name *'Yavana'* had grown to mean uncultured, barbaric people of foreign origin who were always out to wage war, destroy and loot the Indian kingdoms. In one word, *'Yavana'* therefore meant a barbaric enemy. The *'Yavanas'* would come in hordes (armies), attack and kill people mercilessly, pillage and plunder the cities and destroy its life, culture and architecture and go back with a wealth of loot.

In later history (of the period 4th till 13th century) accounts and literary compositions, everywhere such enemies and invaders are thus called *'Yavanas'*. The term has got so entrenched in its latter meaning, that even till date *'Yavana'* find its use as referring to barbaric plundering people, in phrases and folklore.

The later Yavanas in Indian history

Given the expanded meaning, scope and application of the term *'Yavana'* in the later Vedic and medieval period of Indian history (600 – 1300 AD), the term almost became synonymous with the Turkic and Islamic invaders who launched repeated attacks on the Indian kingdoms 1000 AD onwards.

The first of such *'Yavanas'* mentioned in many historical texts, was Sultan Mahmud of Ghazni who attacked the Indian kingdoms and ancient cities and ransacked them during his seventeen invasions of the country. The next famous *Yavana* whose mention we find in historical texts is Muhammad Sihabuddin Ghori who also attacked India multiple times.

There is also historical evidence in the description of the battles of Muhammad Ghori with Jayachandra the King of Kannauj in 1194 AD, where the former is addressed as *"Yavaneswar Sihabuddin"* (The Yavana king Sihabuddin).

Later historians in Sanskrit have continued to address any invader and oppressor thereafter as *'Yavana'*, as we find in ample instances during the wars and annexations done by the Delhi Sultanate rulers. In some much later instances we find even the British being referred to as *'Yavanas'*.

While *Yavanas* do not exist as a tribe neither does their kingdom within any ambit of modern India, the name which started as a reference to the first Greeks of the north-west frontier, lives on in mythological and historical references forever attaching the epithet *'Yavana'* to the sworn enemies of the ancient kingdoms of India.

Zafarabad

The city of present-day Zafarabad finds its origins in the ancient times but offers a chequered history as over time the city changed its character at the hands of many rulers who ruled over it. However, as it never was a city of much strategic or political importance, Zafarabad's name remained low-profile and it was only of any importance to the immediate local region. Zafarabad is situated on the banks of the Gomti River, to the west of Allahabad.

Origins in the ancient times

Zafarabad in the ancient days was a part of the proud kingdom of Kosala and was ruled over by the *Suryavanshi* (Solar dynasty) kings of Ayodhya. At that time the city was called *Manaichgarh*, a name that it carried until it was taken over by the Muslim rulers who changed the name and character of the city. In the ancient times and early Vedic period of history, Manaichgarh was a centre of culture and religion of the Hindus and the Buddhists as established by the ruins of temples and stupas found in abundance in the region.

Early history of Zafarabad

The region flourished under the reign of King Harsha during the 7th century when it came under his empire. After the later

Guptas when entire north and central India was thrown into political chaos, for a brief period, the region was annexed by the Pala kings of Bengal. But they were soon overthrown by the Pratiharas and Bhojas who exercised their control over the region.

The last Hindu king of Manaichgarh was Jayachandra of Kannauj, who is also credited to have built a strong fort here, enclosing eight acres of space to the west of the city. The ruins of Jayachandra's fort can still be seen in present day Zafarabad. After King Jayachandra's defeat and death at the hands of Muhammad Ghori in 1194, the entire region passed under the clamp and rule of his Turkic generals, who completely ransacked the area and razed all religious monuments and buildings, bringing in chaos, destruction and anarchy.

The naming of Zafarabad and its later history

From the time of Muhammad Ghori's conquest till the reign of Sultan Firoz Shah Tughlaq in the Delhi Sultanate, the region came completely under the influence of Islam and gradually began to change its character. It served as an important stop on the route between Delhi and Lakhnauti (Lucknow) and started to grow in importance. In 1321, Zafar Shah was appointed as the governor of the region and he made considerable improvements to the city. It is after him that the city came to be called as 'Zafarabad'.

The advent of the famous Muslim Sufis, Makhdum Sadr-u'd-din (titled *Aftab-i-Hind*) and Makhdum Asad-u'd-din (titled *Chirag-i-Hind*) made Zafarabad an important seat of

Islamic learning and culture. Zafar Shah himself gave the city the name *'Shahr-i-Anwar'* (city of holy lights), but the appellation could not substitute its popular name Zafarabad and the city continued to be known so.

In 1394, the Delhi Sultan Nasiruddin Muhammad Shah (IV) Tughlaq, appointed Malik Sarwar as the new governor of Zafarabad and the adjoining region of Awadh. However, very soon, Malik Sarwar rebelled against the Sultan and proclaimed his independence calling himself *'Malik-us-Sharq'* (the ruler of the east). The dynasty founded by Malik Sarwar which ruled over Zafarabad (and later Jaunpur) was known as the *Sharqi dynasty* and their kingdom the *Sharqi Sultanate of Jaunpur*. The Sharqis ruled over Zafarabad and the region till 1479 when the Bahlul Lodhi defeated the last Sharqi ruler Hussain Shah and the kingdom was permanently annexed to the Delhi Sultanate by Sikander Lodhi.

During the Sharqi dynasty reign, the capital was shifted from Zafarabad to the neighbouring new city of Jaunpur. In 1359, Sultan Firoz Shah Tughlaq had founded the city of Jaunpur and had named it after his brother Muhammad bin Tughlaq whose given name was Jauna Khan. Under the Sharqis, Jaunpur gradually assumed all importance in the empire and once it became the capital, Zafarabad was eclipsed and relegated to being the second city of the Sharqi Empire. However, Zafarabad continued to remain in the glory of its Sufi traditions, music, architecture and also emerged as a major centre for paper manufacturing, for which it also was called *'kagaz ka shahr'*.

The town remained in insignificance thereafter in history and during British India period it was made a part of the

Bombay agency of Kathiawar state, forming a part of the territory of the *Nawab of Janjira*. After independence, Zafarabad was made part of the state of Uttar Pradesh and is today a small town and *'nagar panchayat'* in the Jaunpur district of Varanasi division in the state.

About the author

A post-graduate in English Literature from Kolkata, Sayan is an occasional author and a FinTech corporate trainer by profession. An avid traveller and reader, Sayan's avocation is writing, through which he showcases his own kaleidoscope of life's stories.

Sayan's debut novel *"Friendship Calling"*, was published in 2013, followed by "*A Case of Connections*" in 2016, both novels being based on his true-life experiences. The novels are available on popular book selling portals like Amazon and Flipkart in both paperback and eBook versions and have received wide readership and acclaim.

Sayan also writes articles and short-stories on his blog https://sayanwrites.blogspot.com and as guest writer on other blogs. His short stories have also won the 'Best Short Story in English' award at the 'Srishti Literary Festival', Kerala for three years in a row (2016 – 2018), and the prestigious 'Literati - South Asian Literary Award for Micro-Fiction' in 2018.

Sayan has keen interest in Indian history and mythology and the compilation of this selection on Ancient Cities of India is his first attempt at re-telling and writing based on history.

Sayan can be reached on his email: sayanbhattacharya@ hotmail.com and his Twitter handle @Sayan74.

The End